MW01244519

Copyrigh ____ Paperback
Version This book is a work of fiction.
Names, characters, places and incidents are
products of the author's imagination. Any
resemblance to actual events or locales or
persons, living or dead, is entirely
coincidental. Except for quotes used in
reviews, this book may not be reproduced or
used in whole or in part by any means existing
without written permission from the
publisher, A New Journey Publishing. Do not
redistribute or upload to shared sites. Any
attempt at pirating this work or brand is in
direct violation of the author's copyright. The
unauthorized reproduction or distribution of
this copyrighted work is illegal. No part of
this book may be scanned, uploaded or
distributed via the internet or any other means
of electronic or print, without the publisher's
permission. Criminal copyright infringement,
including without monetary gain, is
investigated by the FBI and is punishable by
up to 5 years in federal prison and a fine of
$250,000. (http://www.fbi.gov/ipr/) Please
purchase only authorized electronic or print
editions and do not participate in or
encourage the electronic piracy of copyrighted
material.

ISBN:979-8-9866029-2-9

I WOULD LIKE TO THANK GOD FOR IF NOT FOR HIM NONE OF THIS WOULD BE POSSIBLE. WOW! I pinched myself my dream has finally come true; it's been a long-time coming baby. This has been a long journey but well worth it. There have been some people that have been there with me while I was going through this journey some have been in my life, and some are new to my life. If I miss anyone who feels they should have mention sorry holla at me and I get you on my next novel. I think I'll start this, this away I would like to thank my dad for being supported of me in all that I do we have been through a lot of hard times, but we are finally on solid ground. I will always be your little girl. I would like to thank my maternal grandmother for teaching me how to be a lady at the time it was a headache but now as a mother and a wife I know how important it is. I would like to thank my two maternal aunts and my four paternal aunts for showing me how strong black woman can make it. I have learned something for each one of you and I want to thank you. I must send out a special thank you to my great aunt Mary she has always been there for me, and I want to thank you. I would like to thank my cousin Pamela and my cousin Felicia these are the first of family that I told I was going to write a book and they both gave me encouragement to take on this journey. I would like to thank my seven heartbeats for asking mommy about her book and being just excited as me. I continue to strive and stay strong for you because you seven are the air I breathe each day and I love each one of you with all that I am. I would like to thank a couple of friends that have been there for me through this journey Yolanda Williams my partner in crime you my girl for life, Patrice Smith friends till the end, Jaleela Ross girl we go wayyyyyyyyy back, Zona Simpson and Eboney Covington nursing school was a bitch but we made it, Latisha Tucker I got faith in you, you can do it, my cousin Tracey Munn Ware girl I could go on and on about what you mean to me but you know that already I love you girl!

I would like to thank my soulmate, my heart, my ride or die words can explain what you mean to me…Always your BABY!!

With Love to All … Letitia Love

Too Good To Be True

By: Letitie Love

Chapter 1

Why did I let Ally talk me into coming out to
the club tonight? I should be home getting
ready for my exam. I've come so close to
getting my high school diploma, I need this.
An opportunity of a lifetime a full tuition paid
to Law School, and the only downfall is they
don't know I have a two-year-old daughter,
Destiny. My sweet Destiny. If they knew, all
chances of going to Law School would be
lost. Professor James has stepped out on a
limb for me in helping me get this
scholarship. He has always said a good mind
is a terrible thing to waste. Why can't that
mean even if you have a child?

"Jasmine!"

"Oh, sorry, Ally."

"Where did your mind go this time?"

"I was just thinking about my exams tomorrow."

"Come on Jazz, you need to relax and enjoy your accomplishments. You're either at school or at your mom's with Destiny. You haven't dated since Damon. He was a jerk so get over it and move on."

"All men are not jerks Jass."

"In whose book, yours or mine Jasmine asked?"

While chitchatting, Jasmine and Ally didn't notice that someone was approaching their table.

"Excuse me, ladies, my name is Malcolm, and I was wondering if you would like to dance," the gentleman said, gazing at Jasmine.

Jasmine was paying no attention to Alicia's hard stares.

"No thanks but my friend, Ally may want to dance."

Malcolm looked at Ally. She was pretty but he really wanted to dance with the beauty he had his eyes on since he walked through the door. Tired of waiting on his friends to get there, he wanted to go ahead and start his night and he wanted it to start with this beauty. However, it didn't seem like it was going to happen that way. It was something about those big brown eyes. They were so hypnotic, but she looked standoffish at the same time. Malcolm had no time for this even though she was fine. He wanted to have some fun tonight and he wasn't going to have it with her, so Ally it would be.

"So, Ally, would you like to dance?" he asked. Ally looked at Jazz and she wanted to yell at her, but that would wait until later. I might as well have some fun while I'm here Alley thought.

"Sure. Why not? Let's burn this dance floor up."

Jasmine sitting at the table alone while nursing her strawberry martini she was thinking to herself again, what am I doing here? That's when Jasmine heard a lot of gasping and whispering, and she turns around and sees what all the commotion was about. I hoped no one is in the club fighting Jasmine thought to herself. I looked around everyone and I gasped myself when my eyes fell upon the most gorgeous chocolate brother I've ever seen.

Smooth skin, light-brown eyes, long eyelashes, long legs, and short curly hair. WOW! Now, that's a nice glass of chocolate milk. I would love to drink that straight down nonstop.

And his legs, they look so strong. Wonder how they would feel under my fingertips while caressing him gently?

Hold the hell up!

Where did that just come from? I haven't thought about sex or had an urge to have sex since Damon.

Didn't have the urge then either. But I fell for the oh-if-you-love-me, you'll-make-love-to-me game. That was two and a half years ago he had his way and stepped, and I ended up with Destiny.

Her name speaks for itself. Haven't heard from his ass since I told him I was pregnant.

His mother apologizes for him, but it's not her fault. She's a wonderful grandmother.

Watching that delicious specimen of a man as all the other women were doing. It was as if he sensed me checking him out, he then looked my way. I swear it was like a lightning bolt hit between us. He must have felt it too because he smiled, and I thought I would come undone right then and there. I knew then it was time for me to go. I can't have any distraction, and Mr. Drop Dead Gorgeous would definitely be a distraction.

Staring at him, I didn't even realize that Alicia hadn't come off the dance floor. She must be having fun. Sometimes I wish I could just let loose and have fun, but I can't. I must work hard and provide for Destiny.

Ally has two parents vying for her attention. She has whatever she wants and needs no matter what the cost. It's hard to believe we're best friends.

We're both from two different backgrounds. She's from a family with a mother and a father, and I'm from a single-family home.

Even though my father is in my life, he also had another family that I sometimes felt I had to compete with for his time.

I remember the first day of second grade, we both were seated at the same table, and we both were new and shy, both loving cabbage patch dolls and being diehard tomboys. We talked in class and on the way home from school. Finding out we lived one block from each other and had many things in common, we instantly became friends. We've been inseparable ever since. Even our parents became the best of friends. Our moms hanging out together and shopping, and our dads playing golf together. Jasmine made her way onto the dance floor.

"Alicia lets go. It's late, and I'm ready to go home."

"Oh, Jazz, just twenty more minutes and we can go."

"Fine. Twenty minutes or I'm catching a cab back home." Walking back to the table, I ordered another drink since I left my other one on the table. I felt like I was being watched. I looked up and there he was, Mr. Tall, Dark and Handsome on his way over this way.

I could hear the ladies behind me whispering. "Girls, Mr. Chocolate is coming our way. Get ready."

I looked up again and realized he was on his way to my table. OH MY GOD! What am I going to say? How do I look? Oh, my goodness! Oh, my goodness!

He just stood there for a second looking into my eyes. Lord, please help me! This man is so fine. Not knowing I was holding my breath, and thinking what am I going to say? As if he had read my mind, he spoke.

"Hello, my name is Emmanuel, and I was dragged out tonight. I was dreading being here but now that I've seen you, I'm glad I came."

Emmanuel didn't want to sound too forward, but he couldn't help himself. She had the most beautiful brown eyes he's ever seen, and he wanted to let her know.

"Has anyone ever told you that you have big beautiful brown eyes? Their sexy and exotic if you don't mind me saying," Emmanuel said.

Jasmine just sat there blushing as he dropped lines hard but that was okay. As fine as he is, he can drop lines all he wants but she won't tell him that.

Besides, being teased as a child for having big eyes, it is always a pleasure when someone compliments them.

"Excuse me," he said. "I didn't catch your name."

"That's because I didn't throw it."

Jasmine didn't mean to say it so harsh. She was just a little nervous. He was making her body do weird things.

Emmanuel looked surprised, from across the room. She didn't look like the stuck-up type, but I guess looks can be deceiving he thought.

He probably would believe that if he didn't recognize that look in her eyes. That hurt, that mistrust of the opposite sex. Emmanuel knew all too well what that look is. He carried it for so long after he ended it with Samantha. So instead of taking it personal Emmanuel wished her a good night and was on my way.

Too bad, she looks like a nice girl. Emmanuel knows how it is when you just don't want to be bothered.

I wanted to scream and tell him to come back. Tell him my name, but I couldn't. Men are trouble and they all want the same thing, but my goodness he was definitely good for a girl's ego.

Just as the thought of calling a cab crossed my mind, I had another thought. Ally must be having one hell of a fun time. She hasn't come off that dance floor yet.

Jasmine decided to go ahead and call a cab, and Alicia walked up.

"What's up, girl? Who was that fine brother you were talking to?" Alicia asked, smiling. "He said his name is Emmanuel, but I told him I wasn't interested, and he left."

"What! Are you crazy, Jasmine! He is gorgeous!"

"I know. Too damn gorgeous. He probably got a woman in at least half the surrounding counties of Cumberland County."

"Jasmine! will you please stop that? All men are not the same. You got to let go of this thing. Damon was one man, and he was young. Damon is not every man. If you keep this up, you'll never meet anyone special."

"Ally, how about we agree to disagree? Are you ready?"

"Just let me give Malcolm my number. He's a fun guy. Maybe he can hook you up with one of his friends."

17

"No thanks. I'm fine, Ms. Cupid."

Jasmine mind drifted back to Emmanuel. I wonder what Emmanuel was doing. Did he find someone to dance with? I know it's plenty of women in here ready to give him a chance. Just as I turned around, there he was with those light-brown eyes focusing on me. Goodness he's handsome as hell, making my clit do double and backward flips, and making me wet just by looking at him. Lord, I'm glad I don't have to see him again.

"Alright, I'm ready, Jazz. Jasmine, Jazzzmen! Damn girl! you should have at least got his number."

"I said leave it alone."

"Fine! That will be you tonight having hot dreams about your stranger from the NCO Club."

I prayed to myself, "I hope not. My exams are tomorrow. No distractions."

Chapter 2

Whoever invented alarm clocks must've had nothing else to do. Why did I let Ally talk me into going to the club on a school night? I wanted to go out and celebrate getting into Pre-law but to the club. UGH!

Jasmine got Shower and dressed; she thought I need to check on my little princess. Jasmine called her mom. Her mom answered on the first ring.

"Mama, how you doing this morning? How's my girl? I missed not seeing her last night. Did she give you a hard time with her bath? I'm going to be late tonight. I got some research to do for one of the attorneys. A family dispute about some land. I just can't wait to start Law School and become a Defense Attorney so I can give Destiny everything she deserves."

"To answer your question, Destiny is fine and you're talking a mile a minute. What's up with you this morning?"

"Finals are today. I'm a little excited."

"I wish we didn't have to hide her in order for you to go to college. I'm so glad Joyce was able to help you get that job at the law firm. It was nice of them to give you a job while you were finishing school. So, if we must keep her a secret for now, that's what we'll do. We do what we must do to make it in this world. You remember that."

"I will. Momma, I love you!"

"I love you too, baby."

Chapter 3

"Hi, Mrs. Jackson," Jasmine said as she walked into the classroom. "I just want to thank you for always being there for me. I took my last exam today. I'm sure I passed it. This is a good program, and without it I wouldn't have been able to get my high school diploma. I will always remember you, especially for putting me in touch with Mr. James. I meet with him today to get the last of my paperwork done."

"You know I'm very proud of you, Jasmine. You have great potential, and I know you're going to be great and do great things in life. Anyway, I can help you, let me know and don't you forget the little people when you hit it big."

"Oh Mrs. Jackson, thank you! I could never forget you."

Jasmine was thinking back to Emmanuel for some strange reason, he looked familiar to me. His eyes have a familiarity about them. Like I've seen them someplace else before. Thinking without looking where I was going, I ran right into a solid chest. I looked up and almost lost my mind. Oh God, it's him. Recognition hit him and he smiled. I could have died right then and there.

"Hi, ah, sorry about that. I wasn't looking where I was going.".

"That's okay," Emmanuel said. "It's nice to see you again."

"Oh sorry, I don't know your name."

"Ah, Jasmine. My name is Jasmine."

"I liked that name. That's my mother's favorite fragrance."

I just looked at him. I could hardly speak and thinking to myself, there he goes again with

23

those lines. Finding my voice, I heard myself say, "Thank you."

"So, are you a student here, Jasmine?"

"Yes, I'm just finishing up in the adult high school diploma program. I'm here to see my advisor. I start school at Duke in the fall."

"I see. I'm here to see my dad. He's an advisor here and we're meeting for lunch. I'm early. I'm going to visit some friends until then."

Feeling her nervousness, he decided to end their conversation. He knew where she would be. He'll find out things he needed to know later. He had a lot of friends at Duke and since he would be teaching there, he knew he would see her again.

"Well, I'll let you go to your meeting. Good luck with your advisor and nice to have seen you again."

Shaking her hand, he tried to hold a straight face because he didn't want her to know how she was affecting his physical being. By the look on her face, she felt it too.

Boy, this is new. I've never felt a connection to a woman like this before, not even with Sharon. God, how I made a mistake getting involved with her. Must have been out of my mind. The question is what am I going to do about this? She doesn't strike me as a girl who wants nothing short of a long-term relationship and really neither did I. So maybe I should just leave this thing alone.

Jasmine walked into her advisor's office.

"Hi, Mr. James. I'm very excited about all this. Going to Law School has always been a dream for me. I'm glad you've found it in your heart to help me. I won't let you down. I'm so ready to go to Duke University School of Law now. That's a mouth full, but it does sound wonderful. My mother is so proud of me. I will be the first to go to college in our immediate family. So, I'm going to make sure I give this my all. I won't let you down."

"Jasmine, I want to ask you something personal. You seem to be so happy about school. I was wondering why you dropped out of school. I mean you've made Dean's List ever since you've been in the Adult High School diploma program. I just don't understand."

Well, there it is. The big question. It's out there. What am I to tell him? Certainly not the truth; I've come too far. I hate to lie to him but too much is depending on this. So, I used the closest thing to the truth.

"Well, Mr. James, my mom got sick, and I had to get a job to help make ends meet."

It wasn't all a lie, Jasmine had reasoned within herself. Mom did get sick, but she got better quick. Early detection caught her breast cancer in the early stages. With chemo and radiation, she was fine, and I was five months pregnant and ashamed. But she stood by my side all the way to the end and told me to always hold my head high no matter what Jasmine thought to herself.

"I'm sorry, Jasmine, I didn't mean to bring up bad memories. I was just wondering what happened. Let's get on with your paperwork for your scholarships."

Great, Jasmine thought. Now I really feel like shit. But this is something that can't be helped. Once I'm done, people will see just because you have a baby, you still can make good choices and make something of your life.

Chapter 4

"Hi, old man, you ready for lunch?" Emmanuel said. "I'm starved. How was your day, anything interesting going on? Do you have many students this semester? You know you're supposed to be taking it easy. Mom won't be happy if she finds out you're working so much."

"I know, son, but your momma got to understand this is my life. I love what I do. I just finished with my last student so I'm ready."

Emmanuel and his dad Walked into Applebee's, all the heads were turning and checking out Emmanuel. Some he knew, and some he didn't. He was popular when he was at DB High School. A big-shot football star, all the girls wanted to date Mr. McBride.

He was quite the ladies' man. But that didn't flatter him; he was into his books.

Girls weren't at the forefront of his mind. He wanted to go to college and be a bigger football star.

"Ally, you know Applebee's is not my favorite place," Jasmine said. "This is supposed to be my celebration. All my paperwork is done, and my schedule is set. My scholarships will be paid first week of school. I can relax for the summer, work at the law firm, and spend some time with Destiny."

 "Hey, Jazz, isn't that your friend from the club?" said Ally, pointing a finger at Mr. Tall, Dark and Handsome. Jasmine turned around in her seat.

"Yes, that's him."

Yes indeed, it was he. He was going to the restroom with all the ladies' eyes following behind him.

"Let's go, Ally. Please. I've seen him once already today. Bumped into him like a Klux. I was so lost for words. I didn't know what to say or what to do. I'll pay if we can just leave. I don't want to see him again."

He does crazy things to my psyche, Jasmine said to herself. Jasmine and Ally left and went to her apartment.

"Okay, Jazz. We're here now so spill it. What's up with you and the guy from the club? What's his name again? Emmanuel."

"Look, Ally, if I tell you this, don't start ragging on me about it, and telling me what I need to do. I just need you to listen without giving me advice. Can you do that?"

"Jazz, I just want the best for you; you deserve happiness just like everyone else. I'll listen without giving advice."

"I've never had such a strong pull toward anyone like this. I mean I think about him night and day. When I think about his strong chiseled face and his gorgeous light-brown eyes, I just don't know how to explain it. I have so much on my plate right now. I'm just scared of getting off track and messing up what I have accomplished thus far. Can you try and understand how I feel? I would love to get to know him, but I'm also scared, because he is so gorgeous, and you know how things go with the good-looking ones?"

"Can I speak now?" said Ally.

"I knew you liked him the night we were at the club. All I'm going to say is everyone deserves to have a little bit of happiness. Do you want to look back one day and wonder what if? I'll support you in whatever you decide to do about dating him, but I do hope you think about it."

Chapter 5

"Mommy! Mommy!"

"Hey, how's momma's little angel? I missed you last night. Have you been a good girl for nana? Hi, mom, sorry about the time. Ally took me out after work to celebrate me passing my finals."

"Don't worry about it; you need to get out more. You be with Destiny every day so don't use her as your excuse not to date or to go out. You will end up resenting her in the long run. "

Jasmine gave her mom a strange look.

"Take that look off your face, young lady. I'll still bend you over my knee." They both burst out laughing. "All I'm saying is it is okay to live a little. Just set standards, and everything will be fine."

"Mom, since it's Friday, I'm going to take Destiny with me so we can spend some time together. I miss her at night. I know we said she would stay here during the week, but I'm missing her more and more."

"Jasmine, I know you miss her but more than anything I think you're lonely. You don't have any adult companionship and I don't mean Ally. You're twenty-three years old. You only had one relationship and you're letting that one relationship turn you against all others. You got to get out and do mingling. I'm not saying you got to jump into something, but at least try and have some fun."

"I hear what your saying momma and I will work on it."

Jasmine told Destiny to get her shoes so they could go home.

Jasmine Kicked off her shoes as she walked into her apartment holding a sleeping Destiny, Jasmine said to herself, "So much for us spending time together tonight."

While Destiny slept in her bedroom, Jasmine felt lonely, and her mind immediately drifted to Emmanuel. I wonder what he's doing tonight. Probably not lying around lonely like me. Maybe Ma is right. Maybe I should get out a little more.

 Before Jasmine could drift off to sleep..He picked her up and gently laid her on the bed not believing that she was finally getting ready to touch him in all the ways she envisioned touching him since the first time she laid eyes on him. His chest broader than she imagined. His skin smooth and soft, like he bathes in baby oil. Hard to believe he ever played football with hands so soft. Caressing her nipples while hard and erect, and just waiting

35

for the touch of his lips. His lips felt so good. Trailing kisses from her soft sweet lips down to her navel; all her nerve endings were on alert. Her panties soaked and wet, and he hasn't even touched my nectar yet. I've never felt like this before. Using his middle and index fingers, he gently stroked her nectar slowly and then faster and faster. Jasmine's body felt things it never imagined it could feel. Her body was floating on air. She was bubbling with anticipation at what would come next when he pushes both fingers inside her wet core. She screamed. She was climbing and climaxing all at the same time, and when she thought she couldn't take it anymore, she rocked against his fingers as she prepared for him to enter her. She was so eagerly awaiting him. Her body was on fire and so he protected them and was about to finally join them and make them as one, but there was a noise. It kept getting louder and louder.

What the hell is that? Drenched in sweat, Jasmine jumped up while the phone was ringing. Her panties soaked. Oh, my goodness, what was that? she thought. Was I dreaming about Emmanuel? I can't believe it. What am I going to do about this?

She was pacing back and forth trying to cool down, but the ringing phone broke her concentration.

Who in the hell can't take the hint about me not answering the phone?

"What is it?" Jasmine yelled into the phone, angrily.

"What's wrong with you answering the phone like that?"

"Who is this?"

"Kaisha! Are you okay? You sound like you're out of breath. Did you finally find someone to end your dry spell?"

"Kaisha, where have you been? I haven't heard from you in a long time. What have you been doing with yourself? Kaisha! What the hell!"

"Oh sorry, Jazz, I was listening to David on the cell phone. I'm back. I've been working at the bank. I'm up for manager. I've been there two years."

"Has it been two years since I've seen or talked to you? You know you wrong for that. We've been friends for at least ten years, half our life and you pull some crap like that."

"I'm sorry, Jazz. After the misunderstanding with Alicia, I thought it would be best if I just left."

"Leaving wasn't the answer, Kaisha. You broke up her and Stephen three weeks before their wedding. All over something you heard. You didn't like her, so you went off, and started spreading rumors and telling her stuff when you didn't have all the facts. So yes, she is a little bitter. You can't blame her. You would be angry, too."

"Jasmine, I just wanted to call and say hello, and let you know how I was doing. I'll be home in two weeks, and I wanted us to get together and go out. Let me know if we can get together. I'll text you my cell phone number."

"Ok Kaisha I look forward to seeing take care of yourself."

They ended their call with an I love you.

Chapter 6

"Hi, beautiful," Emmanuel said to his mother while admiring how lovely his mother has aged with salt and pepper strands in the front, and silvery gray curls cascading down her back. His father had fallen deep in love with his mother the first day he laid eyes on her. "How was your lunch date with your father? I know he's doing more than what he supposed to be doing. I know he enjoys helping his students, but he has to think about his health. We need him just as much as his students. I know that sounds selfish, but I am selfish when it comes to the love of my life."

"You know Dad won't be happy doing anything else. He's been teaching all his adult life. Give him some slack. He won't do anything that's going to jeopardize his health, because you know you're the love of his life, also. Being around you gives me hope of one day being as happy as you are. Maybe finding that special someone."

Geraldine looked at her son and wondered what was going on. He hasn't mentioned being happily ever after before. He hasn't even talked about dating seriously since he and Sharon broke up two years ago. She hurt him badly. I hope she hasn't scared him too much where he won't look for that special someone. He's such a good person. He deserves a nice girl to spend time with. I got a feeling something or someone has piqued his interest. There's only one way to find out.

"What's wrong, Manuel? You're here in the middle of the day and you're talking about finding someone special. Have you met someone?" his mother asked. Emmanuel thought for a moment. His thoughts drifting to Jasmine while remembering those big pretty brown eyes.

Those mesmerizing brown eyes. Her pecan brown complexion. Skin smooth like silk. Sandy brown hair flowing just above her collarbone. She's beautiful as the sunrise on a summer morning.

Geraldine sat smiling and watching her son as the different expressions played across his face. Whoever it is must be something, because she got him looking all glossy-eyed. Hearing his mother call his name brought Emmanuel out of his assessment of Jasmine.

Answering his mother and knowing she wasn't going to give up unless he tells her what's going on. He could never hide anything from her.

She read him like an open book. Not knowing himself how to explain the feelings he was having for Jasmine and being so close to his mother, he knew he could get good feedback from a woman's point of view.

"I went out with Malcolm and a couple of other friends, and I met a girl name Jasmine. She didn't want to talk to me, so she gave me the cold shoulder. Then I saw her again when I went to meet Dad for lunch. She bumped right into me. I was shocked, happy, and nervous. It's just something about her that makes me want to get to know her better, and I haven't felt like this in years. She has this look in her eyes like she's been hurt bad. I just want to get to know her. Do you have any suggestions for me?"

Geraldine sat there speechless and not knowing what to say. She had waited for the day that he would want to start dating again. It's been so long.

"So, you think she's been hurt?" Geraldine said. "Well, if anyone knows how that feels, it's you. And you know how you felt when different women or your friends tried to get you to date. You're going to have to approach her in a different way. Try being her friend and get to know her better.

 Find out her likes and dislikes. Find out who her friends are. You may have to court her the old-fashioned way: slow and easy. If she's truly been hurt, you can't push her. You must take your time. You have a good heart, honey. If you are patient, she will see it too."

Chapter 7

"Good morning," Ally sang into the phone to Jasmine. "How's my precious goddaughter this morning? Are we still on for the fair today?"

"Oh Ally, I forgot all about that but if you want to go, me and Destiny can be ready by twelve."

"Jazz, do you mind if Malcolm comes along with us?"

"Are you two still hanging out together? You must like him. It's been what about three weeks now and you still hanging out? Do tell."

"He's nice. He enjoys talking and he's funny. We go out to eat, I cook for him, and he cooks for me. It's different. I'm just enjoying his company."

"What does he do?" "He's a Computer Specialist for the Federal Government. He's twenty-six, never been married, no children, and he loves his mother."

"Sounds like a keeper." "Even if he had kids, I would still hang out with him. He's just that great."

"At least one of us has a social life. I'm glad I danced with him. I'm just going to take it day by day and see where we end up."

Later that day, Malcolm went to the neighborhood gym to shoot some hoops with his homeboy.

"What's up, Malcolm? What you been up to? Haven't seen you on the court in the last couple of weeks. Where you been keeping yourself, man?"

"I've been hanging out with the girl I met at the club where we went last month."

"She must be special if you're missing basketball games."

"We're just getting to know each other, and she's fun to be around. She can cook, she likes sports, she's intelligent, and she smells so good like sweet honeysuckle, only sweeter. You know the night we met; I had asked her friend to dance but she was cold. So, I ended up dancing with Alicia. I'm glad I did. I didn't realize how beautiful she was until we met the next day for lunch. To say I was speechless is an understatement."

"So, when do I get to meet the lucky lady?"

"We're going to the fair with her friend and her goddaughter. You're free to come if you like."

"You're not going to try and hook me up with her friend, are you?"

"No. I promise I'm through with matchmaking. Be ready at eleven thirty. We're meeting her friend at twelve."

"Why don't we all ride together?" Emmanuel said.

"That's a good idea. I'll call and let her know, and we'll pick them up."

Alicia was singing and dancing. "I'm feeling so good right now. God, if this is a fairytale, please let it last for a long while."

Ally's cell phone rang. "Hey, Al," said Malcolm on the other end. Oh, I just love the way he says my name, Ally thought.

"I was just calling to let you know I invited my friend to go with us. We're going to come and pick you ladies up."

"Hold on, it's Jazz beeping in."

"What's up, Jasmine?"

"Destiny is running a fever. I think I better stay home with her."

"I can reschedule and help you with her."
"No, you go and have fun."

"Look, I'm going to stop by before we head to the fair. I just want to check up on my little lady."

"Okay, see you then."

Chapter 8

'Mommy's little girl not feeling good. Your godmother is coming by to see you and to make sure you're doing okay."

Goodness, she's already at the door. She must have already been on her way, Jasmine thought to herself.

Surprised to see her mother standing at the door instead, Jasmine said.

"What are you doing here momma?"

"I was bored in that house by myself and decided to come and check on my two favorite girls."

"I'm glad you came by ma because Destiny has been running a fever today. I think she is teething. We were going to the fair with Ally and her new boyfriend," Jasmine said, laughing.

"What are you laughing about? You 'bout need one of them for yourself. And why can't you go?" I can keep my grandbaby. Why don't you go out and have some fun?"

"Mom, she's sick. I can't leave her."

"She's probably teething like you said. Now go ahead and call Ally back and tell her you're on your way since the fair is on her side of town."

Jasmine started getting ready while calling Ally at the same time. The phone was just ringing and ringing. Jasmine thought to herself "What's taking Alley so long to answer the phone? Finally, she answered.

"Hello," said Ally is anything wrong?"

"No, I was just letting you know I'm on my way mama came over and she's going to watch Destiny for me."

"Okay, I'll see you when you get here. Malcolm should be here by then. He's picking us up, and he has invited one of his friends to go with us. Is that okay with you?"

"As long as you don't be trying to hook me up. I'm dealing with enough already thinking about Emmanuel day in and day out. I'll see you when I get there," Jasmine said.

Chapter 9

Ally and Jasmine embraced each other in a hug as they always did when they haven't seen each other in a while. They began talking about girly-girl things.

While catching up with each other they never heard a car pull up behind them. Malcolm walked up to Alicia and whispered in her ear.

"What's up, beautiful?" She almost screamed before she saw who it was. Malcolm put his arms around Alley begin to introduce Emmanuel to them.

"Hey, ladies, this is my friend Emmanuel. Emmanuel, this is Alicia and her friend Jasmine."

Jasmine didn't realize she was holding her breath she had been holding it for too long and she suddenly felt as if she was about to faint.

Emmanuel stood there staring at Jasmine with so much desire she could feel it she thought she would blow up in smoke.

This can't be happening Jasmine thought. How am I going to get out of this trip? There is no way I'll be able to spend all day with Emmanuel and not be affected by his presence.

Emmanuel stood there noticing Jasmine's nervousness and remembering what his mother had said to him.

"I can stay. I don't have to go." Emmanuel said., leaving Malcolm in the dark,"

  "What's going on? Did I miss something?"

Malcolm asked, noticing the awkwardness between Jasmine and his friend.

"They kind of met the night we were at the club," said Ally.

Jasmine feeling foolish spoke up.

"It's okay. I'm fine. Let's go and have a good time."

"Are you sure?" Emmanuel asked. "I don't want you to be uncomfortable."

"I'm fine. Let's go."

Jasmine and Emmanuel riding Ferris Wheels and roller coasters, and eating themselves silly, Jasmine had to admit she had a wonderful time with Emmanuel.

He was a perfect gentleman.

I'm more fascinated with him than before, she thought.

He was so sensitive to my fear of heights. If I didn't want to ride something, he would stay with me and keep me company. It was truly a good day. They all had such a great time at the fair.

They all decide to go back to Alicia's house. Jasmine told Emmanuel that she had a good time at the fair.

"I haven't had this much fun in I don't know when." Jasmine said.

"I know what you mean. I haven't laughed so hard in a very long time," Emmanuel told her. "It was a real treat hanging out with you hope we can do it again soon."

Breaking up their conversation, Ally said,

"Seemed like you two had a good time. How about we go to Buffalo Wild Wings and get some drinks?"

Emmanuel looked at Jasmine. Jasmine looked at Emmanuel. Both answered at the same time.

"Not tonight."

Jasmine said, "I got to get home to check on Destiny."

Emmanuel didn't want to put Jasmine on the spot. But he would love to spend more time with her. It was too early.

"Jasmine, we can call Mama and ask her how Destiny is doing." Jazz stood there trying to decide on what to do. She would love to spend more time with Emmanuel, but she was scared. Scared he would try and get close to her, and she wouldn't know how to stop it because he was already getting under her skin. She already knew her dreams were going to be filled with him tonight.

Hearing her name being called suddenly yanked Jasmine back to reality and back to the dilemma at hand.

"Okay, I'll go. I'll call Mama and let her know we're going to get something to eat, and then I'll be home."

Chapter 10

"Momma, I'm home."

"Did you have a good time today, baby?" Jasmine stood there in a gaze. Her mom could tell by the look on her face, but she waited for a response.

"I had a good time, Momma. I'm glad you made me go. I'm thinking about seeing Emmanuel again. I just got to think some things through."

"If you're thinking about seeing him again, he must have made quite an impression so tell me about him."

"He was nice and considerate. You know I'm scared of heights so when I didn't want to ride certain rides, he stayed with me. We talked and found out we have a lot of things in common. I just felt relaxed around him.

But you know I'm scared of getting too involved with anyone, but I am very interested in getting to know him. I just have to take it day by day and see how things go."

Jasmine phone rang.

"Hold on, Momma. Let me get the phone. "Hello."

"Hello to you, too," Ally said, smiling. "Seem like you had a wonderful time today. I couldn't wait to get home so I could call you."

"Yeah, I had a good time. I'm even thinking about seeing him again."

"That would be great. We can double date."

"Okay, calm down. I'm going to take this thing day by day. You know I have a full plate and I can't have too many distractions. But I am going to try this cause girl every time he touched me my pulse rate went haywire.

Alley girl I feel so new at this. I'm like a high school girl on her first date. He even makes me think of doing things I haven't thought of doing before."

"Sounds like you already got it bad for Mr. Tall, Dark and Handsome. You're going to burn up the sheets when the time comes."

I won't, Ally. I've only done it once and it lasted all of five minutes, ten at the most."

"Jazz, he was selfish. He was looking out for himself. All men are not like that, and I really don't think Malcolm or Emmanuel are selfish when it comes to lovemaking."

"Yeah, I agree. That is something else that has me on pens and needles. My inexperience."

"Don't worry you'll know when the time is right, and everything will come natural anyway. I get the feeling he'll lead the way and help you anyway you need help. Just take your time and get to know each other first. All I know is I'm about ready to jump Malcolm's bones even though I know he's trying to be a nice guy."

"Don't hurt the man, Alley."

They both laughed.

"Alley momma about to go I will call you later."

Chapter 11

"Hi, sweetie. I'm home."

"You're thirty minutes late James, and dinner has been ready for an hour. You promised you'd be home in time for dinner. You're supposed to be on semi-retirement but keep staying late for work."

"Geraldine, honey, please try and understand. I do what I do, because I love those kids like they were my own. Some of them don't have the support they need, so I step in and help them the best I can. Come on, sugar. Don't be mad. You know that's why you fell in love with me in the first place. My heart, and oh yeah, don't forget my sexy smile and my sweet kisses."

Geraldine smiled.

"Oh, there we go. That's what I like to see, my angelic smile."

"Okay, James. Just try and be on time for dinner or if it looks like it's going to be a long day, call and let me know so I can push dinner back some."

"Okay, babe. You got a deal. So how was your day today? Did you get many orders for floral arrangements?"

"I had about ten orders today," Geraldine said. "Some going to patients at Cape Fear Valley Hospital Mother Baby Floor, and then some arrangements for funerals."

"Emmanuel came by today. Seems he's interested in a girl he met when he went out with Malcolm. He's very interested in her. I haven't seen him like this since he broke up with Sharon. It was nice to see him into someone again. I thought she had ruined him for future relationships. Glad I was wrong. He asked me for advice, things he can do to win her over. He feels she's been hurt."

"So, what advice did you give, dear?"

"I told him to court her the old-fashioned way. To be friends with her first, and not to push her too fast. For him to let her see that he is a good guy. You know, us ladies like to feel we can trust the people that we're with."

"Well, I hope he is finally interested in someone so he can stop interrupting our secret rendezvous on Saturday mornings," James said, grinning from ear to ear.

"I know babe, but I don't have the heart to turn him away. He is our baby you know."

"Yeah, I know. So is Denise, but she doesn't show up at our doorstep every Saturday for Momma's breakfast. I love my son, but I want my time, too. I want my time to get my grove on, too."

"Oh James, you do know how to make a girl feel good."

"Well then, come over here and give daddy some sugar."

As James was holding and kissing Geraldine, his mind drifted to Jasmine. She was heavy on his mind. He thought about her a lot lately. Since she told him her story, he felt compelled to help her even more. So, he decided to tell his wife about her, but he left out her name.

"Honey, I want to get your opinion on something," James said.

"Sure, go ahead," said Geraldine, listening attentively.

"One of my students, she's very intelligent, full of wisdom, and I met her through Mrs. Jackson, the Director of the Adult High School Program. She also teaches class. She came and spoke to me about this student.

This young lady made straight A's, she was on the Dean's List every semester, and she wants to go to Law School, so I helped her apply for scholarships. I also helped her complete her application. She got accepted at Duke University School of Law Pre-Law program. She was so happy, and so was I. Then I asked her in our last meeting why she dropped out of school? I didn't want to step out of line, but I was curious because she is just that gifted."

"Did she tell you why?"

 "Yes, she did. She said her mother was battling breast cancer, and she had to get a job to help out. I feel so bad for her. I just want to help her in any way I can. I would love for you to meet her. Do you mind if I invite her for dinner sometime soon?"

"Sure, that would be fine. Maybe we could invite Manuel, too. I know he's liking this new person and all. But just in case it doesn't turn out like he wants it to; he'll have a backup."

"No matchmaking, Geraldine. Let him pick his own woman."

"I'm not matchmaking, just being friendly. I promise." She kissed James and they began their dinner.

Chapter 12

"Malcolm, man, I had a good time. You just don't know what you have done for me." Emmanuel said.

"What do you mean?"

"You know that night you met Alicia, I tried to holla at Jasmine."

"I don't have to ask how that went cause believe it or not, I tried to holla at her, too. She turned me down cold."

 "Well, I'm just glad you invited me because I had a chance to show her that I'm a nice guy and I was also able to get her phone number. I'm going to call her tonight."

"Good luck, man. I'm glad she suggested I dance with Alicia, because she is so awesome."

"I think she could be the one for me. I want to take the time out and get to know her. I plan on telling her tonight that I want us to date each other exclusively."

"Wow, man! You really do like her. I didn't expect that from you anytime soon, but I'm glad. You know I believe in one woman at a time. It's too much trying to please two. Why spend all that effort trying to juggle two women when you can put all that energy and time into one woman, and be happy and drama free? And you know I hate drama."

"Well, I'm going to head out. I'm going to stop by and see my parents before I go home. They should be finished with dinner by now."

"Alright, man. Check you later. Let me know how it goes with your phone call tonight."

"Will do. Let me know how your night goes, too." They hugged after their goodbyes.

Ally hadn't realized that her cell phone had been ringing for the last ten seconds it was on vibrate. She looked at the number in her phone and saw that it was Malcolm calling her.

"Hello," Ally answered, smiling.

"Hi there, gorgeous. How are you tonight?"

"You know, Mel," she said, calling him the nickname she gave him. "You are so good for a girl's ego. If I'm so gorgeous, then why don't you make your way over here and show me how beautiful I am?" Shocked at her comment, he just paused for a second.

"Well, let me make myself clear when I say this. You are gorgeous, and when the time comes, I will do just that and more. Believe me, you're going to believe you've died and gone to the heavens of pure ecstasy. Alicia, I know we only been seeing each other for about a month, but I feel like I've known you for years. You're so easy to talk to. We have so much in common. What I'm trying to say is I would like for us to date exclusively."

Speechless, Alicia really didn't know what to say. She knew they had been having a good time together, and she was falling hard for him. She just didn't know he was feeling the same way. Malcolm cleared his throat, bringing Ally out of her trance.

"Are you okay?" he said.

"Yeah, I'm good. You just caught me off guard. I'm glad you feel that way. I didn't want to say anything. I know how some guys are when they think a girl is getting too close too fast."

"So, I guess you can consider us exclusive. When do I get to seal this with a kiss? Alley said.

"If you open your door, you can get it right now."

Ally laughed and proceeded toward her front door. She pulled open the door, and there he was standing in front of her, cell phone to his ear and wearing a huge grin on his face.

"What are you doing here?"

Ally asked. She was so happy to see him.

"I didn't know what your answer was going to be, so I prepared to get on bended knees and beg," Malcolm answered.

"Oh, really? That would have been a sight for sore eyes."

"Come here, girl. Give me my kiss." Lord, kissing this man is driving me insane. She thought to herself. She broke off the kiss before it gets too hot. She knew he wanted to take it slow. In all honesty, she had never been in a relationship like this before when a man wants to get to know you and spend time together before being intimate. Malcolm wanted to give instead of take. What more could a girl ask for?

Chapter 13

After saying good night to her mom, Jasmine had locked the door. Destiny was feeling better now. No more fever. It must have been the teething, Jasmine thought. After giving Destiny a bath and then giving her a snack since she ate all her dinner, Jasmine began to pray to herself.

"Lord, I thank you for her each and every day. She is my rock. Glad you spared your angel to stay here with us for a little while longer. For that, Lord, I say thank you."

After watching Dora and playing peek-a-boo, Destiny soon fell asleep.

"I keep forgetting she is only two and a half years old; she can't last as long as me," Jasmine said to herself.

While reading Trouble Don't Last Always by Francis Ray, the phone rang. Jasmine was so into her book that she didn't hear the phone ringing at first. Looking at the caller ID, she didn't recognize the number at first.

Her book was getting too good. She almost decided not to answer the phone, but then she suddenly remembered that she'd given her number to Emmanuel.

"Hello," he said.

Jasmine said, "Hello" back to him. Softly, her heart was beating a hundred beats per minute. Just the sound of his voice sent chills over her entire body while leaving her with tiny goose bumps.

"Hi, Jasmine. I hope I didn't interrupt you."

"No, I'm good. I was just reading one of my books."

"So, you like to read?"

"Yes, I love to read."

"So do I," Emmanuel said. Shocked, Jasmine said.

"That's great. I don't meet many men who like to read."

"I always have liked to read, but I really got into reading different books while in college. Eric Jerome Dickey is one of my favorites."

"Wow, I like him too," said Jasmine.

"What else do you like to do, Jazz? Is it okay if I call you Jazz? It's so cute."

"Yes, that would be fine." Just listening to her nickname roll off his tongue was making her all hot and bothered.

"I like reading of course, dancing, movies, going out to eat. I study a lot because I'm going to School for Pre-Law in the fall. I work at Briggs and McGirt Law Firm on Breeze

Wood Avenue off Raeford Road. I'm a Legal Assistant with the firm."

"That's great. You have a full plate. You are a very busy young lady."

"And what about you, Mr. Emmanuel? What do you like to do?"

"I like to read as I told you earlier. I like playing basketball with my boys, dancing, movies, and if I had a special someone, spending time with her. Making her smile and keeping her happy. I like watching sports and taking long walks in the park."

"I see we have a lot in common."

"Looks that way, doesn't it?"

Jasmine couldn't explain why she felt so comfortable talking to Emmanuel, but she did. Everything just flowed like they had known each other for years. Hearing

Emmanuel calling her name brought her back into the conversation.

"Where did you go just?" he asked.

"I was thinking how it feels like I've known you for years."

"It does feel like that. I thought it was just me." Emmanuel didn't want to seem pushy, but he desperately wanted to spend more time with her, so he went for it.

"Jasmine, I enjoyed myself today and I was wondering if you would go out to dinner with me tomorrow?"

"I'm sorry. I can't go out tomorrow." Emmanuel took a deep breath.

"I'm not saying no." He perked up then.

"I just can't go tomorrow. I'm going to church with my mom and then afterwards we do an early dinner. If you want to, we can go out next Saturday."

Emmanuel didn't want to wait that long to look into those big pretty brown eyes. So, he took a leap of faith, and hoped he wouldn't push her away.

"Do you think I could come and take you to lunch on Monday?" he asked. "We could go to Casita in Tally Wood Shopping Center."

"That sounds good," Jasmine replied.

"It's a date then?"

"Yes." "I know it's getting late so I'm going to let you get back to your book but before I go do you mind if I call you between now and then. I enjoy talking to you."

"That would be nice. I enjoy talking to you, too."

"Goodnight until tomorrow." Emmanuel hung up the phone. He had taken a long hot shower, he slid into his bed with nothing but what he came into this world with. As soon as his head hit the pillow, his mind drifted to Jasmine.

He couldn't stop thinking about her. Just thinking about her made his manhood rise. He couldn't help but to think about what he would do to her when the time came for them to be together. He could envision it.

The image was so very clear. I would start at her toes kissing them and sucking and licking each one, and not leaving her anything to do but beg for mercy.

Caressing her legs and thighs with my hot wet tongue followed by tiny soft kisses. I'll take my time with her pearl and massage it, massage it until I see her juices running. Then I take my time tasting her with my tongue sliding in and out and making a rhythm only for her. She's opening her legs wide so I can go deeper and deeper. Her legs are shaking, and her body is trembling while her eyes roll in the back of her head. I can tell she's about there. She's shaking uncontrollably. Her body soaked with sweat. I let her catch her breath just for a minute before I let her taste herself from my lips.

I make my way back down to those nice round breasts. Can't forget those as I'm rubbing her hard nipple between my fingers and licking slowly but quickly. I can feel her building up again. She's rolling her hips up and down, back and forward. I give her a little more. I slide one finger in her wet nectar and massage her pearl with the other. After a couple of deep strokes, her juices are running down my fingers. She is screaming my name. After protecting us, I gently enter her while not wanting to hurt her. I could feel the heat and smell her sweet scent. Her body stretched to fit mine. Her moans were getting louder and louder while making me harder, longer, and driving me wild. Going even deeper, we make new rhythms from a mad tango to a slow grind. Her taking, and me giving. She's giving, and I'm taking until we can't take it anymore. She feels so good in my arms. It's almost too good to be true. I'm going deeper. She's opening wider. I can't take anymore. A scream tore from her. And the strongest orgasm I've ever had come roaring over my body. We collapse in each other's arms while looking into each other's eyes. No words were spoken, because none were needed.

Emmanuel woke up drenched in sweat and holding himself.

"That was one hell of a dream," he said to himself. It felt so real as if she was right here with me. If my dream was that hot, I could only imagine how our lovemaking will be simply explosive. I wonder if she's having the same problem I'm having sleeping at night. I can't wait to see her on Monday for lunch. I hope I can get her to go to dinner with me. Lunch and dinner all in the same day, that would be great. Pushing it, but great.

Chapter 14

Monday morning came quickly. Jasmine was excited that she would see Emmanuel again today. It's been one whole day and she already missed him. "I'm getting in over my head with this thing," Jasmine said to herself while driving to work.

"We are not even dating, but just the thought of him makes me dizzy. This is all so new to me." Jasmine thought.

"Good morning, Joyce," said Jasmine as she walked in the office looking dreamy-eyed.

Joyce was the secretary and one of her mother's good friends. Joyce looked at her and spoke.

"Jasmine, why are you glowing this morning? Did Linda forget to tell me something about my goddaughter?" Joyce asked, knowing all along that Linda had already mentioned to her Jasmine's outing with Emmanuel.

"Miss Joyce, she didn't forget to tell you anything."

"Well, child, something's got you floating on air this morning." Jasmine just looked at her and smiled.

"Since you're not talking, your agenda is on your desk. Mr. Briggs left the cases he needed researched inside his office. Looks like you'll be busy today."

"Thanks, Joyce. If I get any calls, just buzz me first and let me know who it is before you put it through." Joyce looked at her strangely but agreed.

Jasmine knew Joyce was going to be on the phone with her mother in a hot second trying to find out what's going on with her. She is so nosey, nosey, nosey, but she means well. I just need a little time to compose myself before I talk to him. I need to get myself together. I don't want to be caught off guard. Hearing someone knocking at the door suddenly grabbed Jasmine's attention.

"Sorry to interrupt but this was just delivered for you."

"Oh, my goodness, they are beautiful! Who are they from?"

"Open the card and see." They both became excited when Jasmine saw who sent her the flowers. She almost fainted. She had never received flowers before this. This was all still new to her. Suddenly, she became panicky. Was this going too far? Was she ready for this? Maybe I shouldn't go out to lunch with him. I don't want to send the wrong impression. Hell, I don't know what to do. I'm so scared of getting hurt or someone getting too close and then rejecting me as soon as he finds out I have a daughter. Risking the wrong person finding out about Destiny. He did say his father was an advisor. What if his dad knows Mr. James? That's it. I won't go. I'll make up a reason why I can't go.

"Jasmine, your friend Kaisha is on the phone," Joyce said. "Lord, not now. I've already got enough on my menu. Okay, put her through. I forgot to call her back.

"Hi, Kay."

"Hi, Jazz. I was calling to let you know that I won't be able to come next week as planned. I got to go to a conference for the bank, but I will be able to come next month. That way, you will have enough time to tell Ally I'm coming because I know you haven't told her yet."

"No, I haven't told her yet but yes, now that does give me some time to tell her. To let her know that you're coming. Hopefully, you two can sit down and work things out." Jasmine looked up at the clock.

"Damn! Kay, I got to go. I'll call you tonight."

I didn't know it was already eleven fifty-five. I wonder if I can catch him in time enough to cancel. Before Jasmine could finish her other thoughts, the telephone intercom began buzzing.

"Jasmine, you have a visitor. He said something about taking you to lunch."

"Let him know I'll be right there."

Jasmine was trying so hard to calm her nerves. "Get it together girl," she said. "You can do this. He's only a man, damn. Yes, a fine man he is. That's the problem. Oh hell. Now, I'm talking to myself." Jasmine opens the door and there he stood talking to Joyce like he'd known her forever. He just has this peculiar charm about him. He turned around with that killer smile, and suddenly Jasmine's knees got weak. She kept finding herself speechless around him. He came over to her and gave her a hug.

You would think that lighting had struck the entire room because their heat was so hot that even Joyce found herself fanning her face. She just turned around and went back to her desk smiling.

Emmanuel looked into Jasmine's eyes and saw all the uncertainty that she has. He knew he had to break down the walls that surrounded her heart and let her know that she could trust him.

"You look nice today," he said.

"You don't look bad yourself, Mr. McBride."

They enjoyed a great lunch at Luigi's.

Back at her office, Jasmine had to admit to herself again that she had a wonderful time and couldn't believe she was going on a date after work. Seeing him two times in one day was making Jasmine giddy. She had to call Ally and give her the update.

"But first, I got to get this work done," she said to herself.

Chapter 15

"Thanks, Ally, for helping me get ready for my date. I'm so nervous. Damon and I didn't go out like this. Emmanuel told me to dress formal so I'm glad you were able to come and help me pick out a dress."

"Jazz, you're going to knock his socks off. You look so beautiful. I've never seen you look so elegant before. Too bad I can't hide in the closet and see his reaction when he sees you. Did you tell Momma you were going out on a date with Emmanuel tonight?"

"You know I did. She is more excited about this date than me. I told her not to get her hopes up. It's just one date. But you know how she does when she's hyped about something."

"I'm going to go now. He'll be here any minute."

"Ally, before you leave, I want to talk to you about something just briefly and then we can finish the conversation tomorrow."

"What's up? You make this sound all serious."

"Well, ummm."

"Spit it out Jazz."

"Kaisha called me today, and she is coming to visit next month. I want you two to sit down and hash this thing out. Y'all are my two best friends."

"Hell no!" Alicia exclaimed. "That's a capital H on that, too. I don't want to see her. If I do, I won't be held responsible for what I might do. And furthermore, she isn't anybody's best friend. She's a user, and she's jealous of everything you do."

"I know you have your issues with her, but will you think about this? We'll finish this tomorrow."

"Okay. I'll hear what you have to say, but I never want to be friends with her again. See you later, girl."

Just as Ally was opening the door, the doorbell was ringing.

"Hi, Emmanuel. Bye, Emmanuel."

"Ah, you don't have to leave."

"Yes, I got some errands to run. You two have a good time." Emmanuel looked up as Jasmine had looked up at him. He was stunned. He knew she was beautiful, but Good Lord, help me. Her skin is so flawless. Her eyes are shining bright. That purple dress she's wearing is hitting every curve she has. She has definitely given the Coca-Cola bottle a run for its money. I'm going to need some help tonight. I haven't been in the company of a woman in two years, and this beautiful creature before me has me salivating at the mouth. He thought to himself.

Jasmine could see the desire in his eyes. She couldn't believe he was looking at her like that. She never considered herself as a looker, but the way he was looking at her was making her tingle all over.

I just can't get over how this man makes my body react. It's just purely sinful. Emmanuel broke into her thoughts.

"Jazz, you are the most beautiful woman I've laid my eyes on." Jasmine couldn't do anything but blush. He saw her blushing, and then rubbed his finger down her cheek. He felt her tremble, and he knew then that he affected her just as much as she affected him.

That was a good thing to know. For a moment, they just stood there looking into each other's eyes as if they were searching for each other's souls. Emmanuel, breaking their connection again, asked,

"Are you ready to eat? I can't wait to be seen with you on my arm." Jasmine just shook her head and giggled a little. This is going to be an eventful night, Jasmine thought.

"So, where are you taking me?" Jasmine asked.

"We're going to this place called A Little Taste of Jazz. It's a new jazz club. My buddy opened it, and its formal night for the grand opening. I'm going to have to keep you close, because of that dress you got on. I wouldn't want to have to jack someone up for hitting on you."

Jasmine swayed back and forth to the music. She was having the time of her life. The dinner was exquisite: rack of lamb, red potatoes, and cream butter corn with homemade biscuits. It was the bomb. Emmanuel did mingle a little, but for the most part he didn't leave Jasmine's side for too long just as he said he wouldn't. When they opened the dance floor, Emmanuel could tell Jasmine wanted to dance so he took her hand and they hit the dance floor.

Emmanuel was in for a real treat with the way she was moving her body on the dance floor. She had set his manhood on full alert, and her body was talking to him. His body was listening. He could barely keep up with her. He would've never imagined she could dance like this. They stayed on the dance floor dancing up a storm all night until they both became tired and decided that it was time to go.

Standing at Jasmine's front door, she asked Emmanuel. "Would you like to come in for a little while?"

"Sure, that would be nice." He took her keys, and let them in.

"I'll be back. I'm going to change into something a little more comfortable. Make yourself at home." Emmanuel turned her stereo on and then put in a jazz CD.

He sat patiently for her to return. Several minutes later, Jasmine came back with her Duke shorts on and a tank top not even realizing how sensuous she looked. She sat down next to Emmanuel not noticing the hard on he now had.

"Emmanuel, I had a wonderful time. How can I repay you for such a good time?"

"Promise me that we'll do it again," was his only reply.

"Okay, I promise."

"Jazz, it's getting late, and I should be going. I know you have to work tomorrow."

"Okay," she said softly. She knew he had to go. She just didn't want the night to end so soon. "I'll call you tomorrow." She walked him to the door. He looked at her and gave her a kiss on the cheek. She felt a light burning sensation on her cheek from his kiss.

He then turned to face her and to say good-bye when suddenly she stepped up, wrapped her arms around his neck, and started kissing him while pushing her tongue past his lips.

She was kissing him with such passion. He was squeezing her as his hands were palming her ample behind, and she was grinding into his erection. She was breathing heavily. She could feel her nectar getting wet. She was surely dripping. He took his fingers and slipped them into her shorts. He could feel her wetness and became even harder.

Jasmine didn't know what had come over her. Was this her inner vixen coming out? She was tugging on his shirt. She almost got it over his head when he stopped her.

Emmanuel had to dig deep for his will power. He needed it now more than ever. She wasn't ready for this. She was just caught up in the moment. He couldn't. No, he wouldn't do this. He wanted a relationship with her. Yes, he wanted her body, but he knew now that he also wanted her mind, body, and soul. So, he stopped her. Jasmine gave him this funny look, because she thought he was rejecting her.

"Listen to me," Emmanuel told her. "I feel like I've known you for years, and I'm finding myself caring for you a great deal. I want you. God knows I do, but when we take that step, I want you to be sure. I don't want you to wake up with regrets. When we come together, I want it to be special in every way because I want your mind, your body, and your soul. Can you understand what I'm saying?" She just sat there shaking her head, because at that moment she knew that

Emmanuel McBride would have her heart. He gave her another kiss, and they said their good-byes. Jasmine floated upstairs to her bed. She was ready to fall asleep because she knew her dreams would be filled with thoughts of Emmanuel.

Chapter 16

Jasmine suddenly woke up to a ringing phone. Looking over at the alarm clock, she knew it couldn't be anyone but Ally.

"What you want, chick? You are calling to be nosey."

"No, I just wanted to hear your voice this morning." Jasmine looked at the phone. "Oh goodness, I feel so silly. I should've looked at the caller ID," she said, hearing Emmanuel calling her name.

"Oh sorry. I wasn't expecting you. Ally is usually the only one that calls me this early."

"I'm sorry. Did I wake you? I can call you later."

"No, you're fine. I'm just a little surprised, but it's a nice surprise."

"I was wondering what you are doing after work?"

"I'm going to visit my mother. Why, did you have something in mind?"

"Yes. I thought maybe we could go to a movie."

"I can't go to the movies but if you can wait until I finish visiting my mother, you can come over. We can watch a movie and pop some popcorn." Emmanuel really didn't want to be alone with Jasmine. Being scared that he wouldn't have the strength to turn her away two days in a row, he still agreed anyway.

"Okay, that's cool. Just call me when you leave your mom's, and I'll meet you at your place. Do you need me to bring anything?"

"No, just you." "Well, I'll see you tonight."

"Okay." Before Jasmine could get into the shower, her phone was ringing again. This time, she did check the caller ID. This time, it was Ally.

"What's up, girl?" "Did you give up the goods?"

"Say what!" "I'm just playing, Jazz. I know you didn't do anything." The line suddenly went silent, and Alicia yelled.

"Oh my God! Jasmine, you did give up the goods. Tell me everything. Was it good? Did he cum fast? Did he make you scream?"

"Alicia, are you going to let me answer any questions?"

"Oh sorry, go ahead."

"No, we didn't have sex." "Oh man, I was getting happy for nothing. Somebody got to be getting something."

Jasmine whispered, "It wasn't from lack of trying."

"Excuse me, but what did you just say?"

"Nothing!"

"You better come better than that. What do you mean not from lack of trying? Spill it. Come clean now or you're not getting off this phone."

"Alright, girl. Everything was going well, but then he kissed my cheek. I got warm and fuzzy all over. Then something came over me, and I started kissing him on the lips. I stroked his tongue, and he returned the favor. We were getting carried away and before I knew it, I was trying to pull his shirt off. He was hard as a rock, and I was wet. I mean I was soaked, but he stopped us. I was offended at first, but then he made it clear why he stopped. He said he wanted to wait; that he wanted me to be sure. He wants my mind, body, and soul. Girl, I thought I was going to jump his bones all over again. I'm trying not to fall for him, but he's making it very hard. He is so damn nice."

"Girl, tell me about it. Malcolm is the same way. Maybe we've found ourselves a couple of good guys."

"Well, I got to go get ready for work. Let's meet for lunch so we can finish the discussion about you and Kaisha getting this stuff settled between you two."

"Okay, that's fine. We might as well get this out, so I won't have to hear that skank's name again," Alicia said.

"I might as well go ahead and call Momma before I go to work," Jasmine said after she placed her phone's receiver back in its cradle.

While waiting for her mom to answer the phone, Jasmine couldn't help but to think how Emmanuel was going to act when he found out about Destiny. Would he not want to see her again? I guess only time will tell. Jasmine smiled when she heard Destiny answer the phone. She could hear her mother in the background telling Destiny, "That's your momma. Tell her good morning."

"Good morning," said Destiny.

"Hey, Destiny. How's my little lady this morning?"

"I love you, Mommy," Destiny kept saying repeatedly. "I love you too, Dee," Jasmine said, calling her little girl by her nickname.

Destiny laughed like she didn't have a care in the world. It was times like these where Jasmine missed her baby so much. I'll be so glad when all this is over, she said within herself.

"Let me speak to Grandma, Dee." The phone line went silent until, "Hello," was uttered.

"Good morning, Mom. How are you doing this morning?"

"Shouldn't I be asking you that, Ms. Thang? You're the one who went on a hot date last night."

"Oh Mom, I had a great time. He is such a gentleman. I am so scared, but he makes me feel wonderful."

"That's a good thing, Jazz. Just take things slow and easy and see where things go."

"Mom, I haven't told Emmanuel about Destiny yet. I wanted to wait and see how things are going to turn out before I tell him. I hope he doesn't run away when I tell him. He doesn't seem like the type that would do that. I guess I'll just have to wait and see."

"I understand why you didn't tell him about the baby. Don't worry yourself. I know you want to be sure before you bring someone into Destiny's life. If he's the man he seems to be so far, you'll be okay."

"Momma, I'll see you and Destiny this evening. Thanks for the talk. I love you, Momma."

"I love you too, baby." As Jasmine was getting ready for work, thoughts of Emmanuel crept into her mind again. She smiled. This was so new to her. She felt very good inside. "I like this feeling," she thought to herself. I'm looking very forward to seeing him again tonight. "Alright, little Ms. Vixen. You better behave tonight, no being naughty. I don't know what has gotten into you lately. Yeah, the hell you do! That fine ass specimen of a man named Emmanuel. That's what's gotten into you. That's the whole problem. Yes indeed. Lord, now I'm talking to myself again. What's next?"

Chapter 17

Before Jasmine could get both feet in the door, Joyce was in her face.

"So, how did it go last night? Did you have a good time? Are you going to see him again?" Joyce asked. "What is it with y'all this morning?

"You know you already know what happened. You just don't want me to be suspicious if you didn't ask me any questions. You and Momma are not slick."

"Okay, you got us, but I still want to know. I mean you must have had a good time with that big vase of red, yellow, and pink roses in your office. I would say you had a killer of a time." Jasmine sprinted to her office, and she couldn't hide the smile. Her face simply glowed with happiness.

"Oh, my goodness! I can't believe he sent me flowers again today, and such a beautiful arrangement. I'm going to have to call and thank him.

"Auntie Joyce, what am I going to do? He's making it hard for me to not fall head over heels."

"Listen, Jazz. Just take your time and enjoy yourself. If it's meant to be, it will happen. If not, you will know that too. Don't start getting all jittery and doubting whether you should see him or not. Now, go on in there and call that man," Joyce demanded.

As Jasmine was about to call Emmanuel, her cell phone started ringing. She looked at the caller ID. Kaisha had very bad timing. "Hello."

"Hi, Jazz. I wanted to let you know I will be finished earlier than expected. So, I'll be home at the end of this month. Hopefully, we will be able to get together. I really do miss you."

"Okay, Kaisha, that will be fine," said Jazz.

"I'm meeting with Ally today for lunch. We're going to talk about this thing the two of you got going on. I can't make any promises, but I hope I will be able to get through to her, because I don't want to have to choose between the two of you when you get here. I'll call you later this week and let you know how things go. But until then, take care of yourself."

Jasmine sat thinking back to when her and Ally met Kaisha at the skating rink while chilling and hanging out and thinking they were the best thing since sliced bread, they quickly took notice of Kaisha. She seemed to be all alone, and since they knew how that felt, Jasmine told Ally that she wanted to invite her over to hang out with them. Ally got so excited about that idea, and they asked Kaisha to hang out with them. We found out that she went to our school, and she became our friend. The Three Musketeers are what we called ourselves. As time went on, we learned that Kaisha had a jealous streak, but she was an underdog, and I was always a sucker for the underdog. We continued to be friends with her anyway despite things we didn't like about her. Ally was always somewhat leery of Kaisha anyway, and now I'm wondering how I am going to fix this mess between them as if I didn't have enough myself to deal with already. Ally really can't stand Kaisha now, so it is going to be very interesting to see how all this turns out.

Jazz's cell phone began ringing.

"Goodness, this is a hot line today," she said. Before answering her cell phone, she looked at her caller ID to see who it was that's calling her. Hoping that it would be her sexy Emmanuel calling her, she was a little disappointed when it wasn't him.

"Hi, Ally," Jasmine said.

"Are we still on for our lunch date? I'm looking forward to a great lunch, Jazz, but I'm not looking forward to talking about Kaisha. I can't stand her and nothing you can say will change that, but we will talk and get this shit on the table once and for all."

"Meet me at Olive Garden at one thirty," said Jasmine. "And Ally, please bring an open mind."

"Whatever, I'll see you then and I want to know all about Mr. Emmanuel and what you've been up to," Ally whispered before hanging up.

Jasmine was looking around her office and thinking how good it would be when she becomes an attorney. Because of Mr. James and his great advice, she thought, I took college classes while getting my diploma and now I only have one year of undergrad school to go. Then I'll be doing that while starting my law classes. I guess it does pay to be a little smart. Thinking to herself.

Her mind drifted back to Emmanuel, and she began thinking how good he made her feel. She was looking forward to seeing him tonight. Just thinking of him made her remember she didn't call him and thank him for her flowers. Then she had a better thought, No. I'm not going to call him. I'm going to send him some flowers. I know he will be surprised to get some red roses from me. I know that will throw him off kettle a little bit. She found a florist and made the call.

"Geraldine's Arrangements, how may I help you?"

"Yes, I would like to order two dozen of long stem red roses, and I would like to have them delivered," said Jasmine to the woman on the other end of the line.

"Would you like a card to accompany your order?"

"Yes, that would be nice. How about thinking of you always?"

"And who is the lucky fellow?"

"His name is Emmanuel, and his address is 2325 Hilltop Drive, Hope Mills, N.C. 28368," said Jasmine, who was so happy at the prospect of sending her man flowers. She was so happy but also fidgety at the same time.

Geraldine had gasped and cleared her throat before Jasmine picked up on it. Then she began wondering whom this young lady was sending her son flowers. Two dozen of red roses at that! Could this be the young lady he told her about? Geraldine thought. Or is this someone else trying to get his attention? She had to know but she relaxed, because she knew she had to give me her name and credit card number in order to be billed. So, Geraldine waited patiently until she gave her credit card number, and her name it indeed was the young lady he told her about, Geraldine thought to herself. Geraldine became so excited she decided to give the young girl a discount. She quickly made something up about 'a special of the day'. It went off without a hitch.

 Emmanuel must be making progress. She's sending him roses, and two dozen! Wow! They finished completing the order and said their good-byes, but not before Jasmine thanked her for her service. Geraldine thought to herself again, "And she has good manners. Yes! I like her already!"

Chapter 18

Emmanuel quickly ran to answer his ringing doorbell. When he had opened the door, he was surprised and couldn't believe his eyes. Two dozen of red long stem roses, and they were delivered from his mom's shop. Knowing his mother, the way that he knew her, there would be questions to answer when he saw her again. Questions that he wasn't ready to answer yet, because he wasn't sure himself. He wasn't going to worry about that right now. He just wanted to call Jasmine and thank her for the roses. He knew without even looking at the card that they were from her. He could just feel it. Jasmine was so engrossed in her work that she almost didn't hear her phone ringing at first.

"Hello," she said, without looking at the caller ID. She was trying to get ahead in her work. She knew her lunch with Ally wasn't going to be easy.

"Did I disturb you?" Emmanuel asked. She just sat there and smiled for a minute while trying to get her breathing under control.

"Hey, are you there?"

"Yes, I'm here," said Jasmine.

"I just wanted to call and thank you for the roses. They're nice."

"Just a thank you for my arrangement. They were more than nice; they were exquisite."

"I'm looking forward to us spending time together tonight," Emmanuel said.

"Same here," Jasmine replied.

"Well, you get back to work and I'll see you tonight."

While getting ready for her lunch with Ally, Jasmine heard her cell phone ringing again.

Looking at the caller ID, she noticed it was Kaisha again. "Lord, what now?" she thought.

"Hi, Jazz, sorry to keep calling but they have changed my schedule again. They stuck me with training a new girl, so I have to get her ready before we start traveling to the other branches. Looks like when I come home, I will have to do some work there because the new girl will be relocating there.

So, it will be the end of next month before I come. This will really give Ally a chance to cool down a little more. I'll be in contact with you. Take care."

"You take care too, Kaisha."

Chapter 19

Before Jasmine could even sit down, Ally was already saying, "Let's get this out of the way now before we order. I don't want this upsetting my appetite." Jasmine just sat there for a moment to get her bearings.

"Look, I don't want to play referee between the two of you when she gets here. Can't you just try? It's not like she's going to be staying here."

"Thank goodness for that blessing," Ally whispered.

"I heard that," Jasmine said. "Come on, let the past be the past so we can just get past this for me at least."

"I'm going to make this simple for us and this is only for you. Don't make any mistakes in thinking this is for Kaisha," said Ally while smiling just a little.

Could this be my lucky day? Jasmine thought.

"Look, when Kaisha comes into town, I will be cordial towards her. I will go out with y'all twice, and maybe we can chill at the apartment once or twice and that's it. Don't ask for more. I'm only doing this for you as I said before. Take it or leave it." Jasmine thought she would jump out of her seat at what Ally said.

This was better than anything she could have asked for, Jasmine thought. Jasmine wasn't going to push her luck. She did have a little time before she had to deal with the both of them.

"Can we eat now?" Ally asked. "Now that that's out of the way, how are things going with you and Emmanuel?"

"Things are going good," Jasmine answered with a goofy look on her face. Alicia couldn't do anything but smile. She was so happy for Jazz.

"He's coming over tonight to watch some movies. I just hope I can keep my hormones under control. It's just something about being around him that makes me want to touch him all over. Jump his bones would be more like it."

"I hear you on that. High five to jumping bones," they both said, laughing.

Jasmine was back at her office finishing up the last of her work, she called her mom to let her know she would be on her on way.

Jasmine headed to her mom's she was Listening to her Mary J. Blige CD, she just wanted to unwind a little before she got to her mom's house.

While driving, Jasmine quickly visualized how it would be when she could afford to put her and Destiny in their own house. Destiny's room would be decorated with Dora, which she loves so much along with all her stuffed animals. She could hardly wait. Jasmine knew this journey wasn't going to be easy, but she was determined to get this done.

Using her key to let herself into her mom's place, she didn't see or hear Destiny or her mother. Jasmine called out but there was no answer. She walked further into the house and that's when she saw her mom and Destiny playing in the back yard, and for a quick second she was consumed with jealousy. But as quickly as it came, it went away. She knew where she stood in Destiny's heart. This is something that must be done.

"Mom, I'm here," Jasmine called out, as she walked into the back yard. Destiny came running just as soon as she heard her momma's voice.

"Mommy!" Destiny sang out. "I love you, mommy!"

"I love you too, princess." At that moment, Jasmine knew without a doubt where she stood in her baby's heart. Her greatest fears were that Destiny would get attached to her mother and push her to the side. But at this very moment, Jasmine knew that things would be alright.

Chapter 20

After spending a little time with her mother and Destiny, Jasmine made her way toward home. She was so excited about seeing Emmanuel tonight. She already had the movie ready, some wine chilling in a bucket of ice, and some cheese and crackers. Thank goodness for Rachel Ray. She'll help a girl throw something together in a flash.

Rushing into her apartment, Jasmine was moving fast because she wanted to take a shower. She wanted to be nice and fresh for Emmanuel when he arrived. Jasmine was setting the wine glasses on the table when the doorbell suddenly rang. "Okay, Jasmine, calm down and get your bearings together," she said to herself.

Jasmine, opening the door slowly, saw a yellow rose being pushed toward her through the small opening by none other than Emmanuel. She opens the door the rest of the way, and in walks Emmanuel with that swagger that seems to drive her insane. He gave her a peck on the cheek, and suddenly she felt herself getting warm all over. Emmanuel felt her tremble.

He didn't know how he was going to handle being here alone with her again tonight. So, he decided to do what he does best; play it safe.

"What are we watching tonight?" Emmanuel said. Jasmine gave him a sly grin.

. "I know what that mean?" Emmanuel said, "A girl flick."

"One of my favorite movies I may add," said Jasmine. "Fools Rush In." Emmanuel laughed because his sister Denise liked that movie, too.

He sat down while Jasmine got the wine and cheese, and they began to watch their movie. It had only been one hour into the movie, and they both were laughing hysterically and having fun. Jasmine laid her head on Emmanuel's shoulder, and the next thing she knew she was fast asleep. Emmanuel looked down and saw she was asleep. He was going to try and move away, lay her down, lock up, and leave. She must have had a long day, he thought. Just as Emmanuel was about to move her, he heard her whisper his name. Then a moan followed, and he instantly became aroused. Now, he knew that he wasn't alone when it came to those sleepless nights. Emmanuel, still trying to get up, felt Jasmine move closer to him. Rolling over, she suddenly opened her eyes and realized she was lying in Emmanuel's lap. Jasmine felt a little embarrassed that she'd fallen asleep on him. She knew it had to be the wine, because she was not a drinker.

"Emmanuel, I'm sorry I fell asleep on you. I think that nap gave me a burst of energy."

"Jasmine, I think I'm going to head on home so you can get some rest," Emmanuel said.

"We can get together this weekend if that's okay. I'll be calling you all week, though. I can't go without hearing that sweet voice of yours." Jasmine stood there blushing

. She said, "Okay, do a girl at least get a kiss good night?" Jasmine could neither explain nor understand what happens to her whenever Emmanuel is around.

She just felt so comfortable around him, and she wanted him touching her all the time. "Goodness, what just came over me?" she thought. Hearing Emmanuel calling her name snapped her right back to the reality of getting her good night kiss. Emmanuel was thinking long and hard, because he knew if he touched Jasmine, he would have to fight with his inner self again tonight. But if his Jasmine wanted a kiss, then a kiss is what she would get. He'll just have to go home and take a cold shower.

He reached for Jasmine and pulled her close to him. When his lips touched Jasmine's, he knew that he was in trouble. She slid her tongue through his lips, and he thought he was going to come undone. She was moaning or was that him moaning?

Jasmine's hands were all over him, and his hands were all over her. She was unbuckling his belt. Before he knew it, he had lifted Jasmine up off the floor and had her back to the wall. She was pulling at his shirt. He stopped and cursed under his breath, "Not again."

"Oh, Emmanuel, please don't stop. I want you now. I don't want to wait."

Emmanuel knew he couldn't reject her two nights in a row. He knew her hormones were on the rampage because his were, too. They were like gas and fire, combustible.

He wanted to please her and make her feel special. He'll let the cold shower ease his aching, throbbing nature when he gets home tonight. Without speaking, Emmanuel laid Jasmine down on the chair while trailing hot kisses down her neck and stopping only to nibble on her breast. First, the right. Then, left. She jumped when he nibbled and licked on her right nipple. He knew then her right nipple was more sensitive than the left, so he stayed there a little longer. Looking down at her, he knew she was enjoying herself.

Emmanuel continued kissing Jasmine down her stomach and removing her gym shorts along with her black lace panties. He rubbed her pearl, and he could feel that she was already very wet. He wished he could make love to her right then, but it wasn't time yet. His plan was to please her and go home. She didn't know that, but she was about to find out. Jasmine was thinking to herself, Lord, I've never felt like this before. I am so glad Ally talked me into getting these sexy panties.

I am so ready for him. I can't believe I want to give myself to him. It just feels so right. Jasmine jumped when she felt Emmanuel slide two of his fingers inside of her. He was stroking her with his fingers. Jasmine was moving her hips to match the motion of his fingers. She was starting a groove when he slowly pulled out his fingers. She was about to protest when she felt something wet run across her clit. Then it pushed inside her. She screamed a little and tried to scoot away, but before she could move Emmanuel had grabbed her by the waist and pulled her back. He licked and sucked and stroked her with his tongue.

Her juices were flowing and running everywhere. "Ummm, she tastes so good," Emmanuel thought to himself. Jasmine felt she would faint at any time now.

She has never had this feeling before. Her legs trembled. Her clitoris was sensitive every time he stroked it. She felt like she was being lifted off the floor. Is this what an orgasm feels like?

She felt this wonderful feeling, and it kept getting stronger and stronger. She couldn't do anything but rock with him until finally it felt like something had exploded. She screamed Emmanuel's name to the top of her lungs.

She couldn't move at all. All Jasmine could do was lay there. Emmanuel was so happy to see that glow on Jasmine's face. He was happy to know he was the one who put it there. So many times, he wanted to protect them and slide between her pecan brown thighs.

But this was her time. If he were a guessing man, he would think that she hasn't done this before, Emmanuel thought. Another reason to wait is he needed to know if Jasmine has had sex before.

She felt mighty tight when he slid his fingers in her. Can't be, he thought, looking up at her again. He saw that she was almost asleep again. He kissed her on the lips.

"Hey, sleepy head."

"I'm not sleep," Jasmine said. "I'm just relaxed. I really can't explain how I feel. Never felt like this before." Emmanuel was feeling more and more that he was right. He didn't want to just come out and ask her. He would have to tread these waters lightly.

Jasmine was giving him that look like what's next?

Emmanuel said, "Did you enjoy yourself?" She blushed while shaking her head up and down and feeling a little embarrassed about acting the way she did. She didn't know the correct way to act. This was all new to her.

Since she felt like she could talk to Emmanuel, she told him what she was feeling.

"Emmanuel," Jasmine said.

"Yes, baby." She smiled. He called me, baby, she thought. "Are we going to make love now?" He smiled at her.

"No, baby, we're not. I still want us to wait." She looked at him confused.

"But what about what you just did? I thought…" He stopped her and said.

"That was for you. I enjoyed making you feel good. It makes me feel good to make you feel that way. Our time will come soon." Jasmine looked at Emmanuel and said.

"Manuel."

"Yes, sweetie." "I have to tell you something. I'm new to this. I've only been with one person one time, and it lasted about five minutes. So, these feelings I have are new to me. I had no idea it could feel like this." I see what all the hoopla was about, she thought to herself. "I'm going to need you to be patient with me.

"When the time does come, believe me you'll know it." He looked at her and ran his finger down her cheek. "You're going to be just fine. It's getting late. I better go. You got to work in the morning, and I'm going to visit my mother in the morning."

They kissed and said their goodbyes.

Driving home, Emmanuel thought to himself, I can't stand a selfish man. He was given something precious and didn't even know what to do with it. That's okay, though. I'll make sure she knows how wonderful it can be when two people come together as one."

Chapter 21

Two months later, Jasmine and Emmanuel were still spending time together and getting to know each other better. Kaisha was due to come in a couple of days. Everything was going well.

Jasmine decided it was time to tell Emmanuel about Destiny, and if everything went okay, she didn't want to wait any longer. She would make the first move. Her body now ached for Emmanuel. Every time they touched or kissed, she wanted him more and more.

She had to get this secret off her chest and out in the open so they could move forward. If everything went as planned, she didn't know how she was going to accomplish getting her apartment together and going shopping. Right then, she had a thought. "I'll just get Ally to help me," she said to herself.

Emmanuel thinking to himself, this has been the best two and a half months ever. I don't think I believed in love at first sight until I met Jasmine. I've had her all to myself, and now my parents, well I will say my mother is pressuring me to bring her to dinner. We agreed to get to know each other better before we started bringing family into our relationship. Things are good between us, and we're getting more serious every day. So, I will bring it up tonight about meeting each other's families.

As soon as Jasmine got into the office, the first thing she did was tell Joyce to hold all her calls. "I have some planning to do. she told Joyce.

Just as she was about to sit down, Attorney Briggs walked in. Jasmine looked up when she heard her door open, and she greeted him with a soft smile.

"Hey, Mr. B," she said. That was the name he insisted she call him.

"Jasmine," he said. "I know we've been keeping you busy lately."

"I love what I do. You know that."

"I know. That is why it is so easy for us to love and depend on you. I know we bypass each other day by day, because we're always in court. But we have a surprise for you." She looked a little shocked, and said, "A surprise?"

"Yes, we're sending you and a guest on a seven-day vacation anywhere you want to go. You get to call the agent and make all your arrangements." Jasmine just stood there with her mouth open. She couldn't believe her ears. He laughed at the expression on Jasmine's face.

"Why do you look like that, Jasmine? You know you mean a lot to us. This is for getting your high school diploma while taking college classes and getting into Pre-Law school and working for us at the same time. That's a great accomplishment."

"Thank you," was all she could say without bursting into tears.

"Carlos saw how emotional Jasmine was getting and he excused himself, so she could get herself together and so he could get himself together.

Jasmine had called Ally on the phone while fighting to hold back tears but losing the battle. Ally, answering the phone and hearing sniffling on the other end, Alley said, "Jasmine, is that you?"

"Yes," Jasmine said, wiping tears away from her eyes.

"What's wrong? Did something happen to Destiny?"

"No, I was crying but they were tears of joy."

"Come again?" Ally asked.

"Girl, you won't believe what just happened!

Mr. B just gave me a seven-day vacation anywhere I want to go with all expenses paid!"

"What!" Ally exclaimed. "Girl stop lying!"

"I'm flying if I'm lying, and you know I haven't flown nowhere. I was so surprised. It just made me cry to know that they cared that much. It made me feel very special. Girl, that isn't all. I get to take a guess."

"Wow. Now that's something. Glad I'm your best friend."

"Hold it. I don't know whom I'm taking or when I'm going. So don't get all happy."

Jasmine and Ally chit-chatted for a little while longer before Jasmine told her, "I'm going to tell Emmanuel about Destiny tonight. If everything goes like I hope it will, I also plan to make love with him tonight." Ally was quiet for a minute.

"Are you sure you're ready for this?"

"Yes, I'm very sure."

"Okay, if you're sure, then I'm behind you one hundred percent." Jasmine cleared her voice, and right then Ally knew she wanted something.

"Okay, what you want, Jazz?" "I need help with setting up everything with Emmanuel. I want some sexy lingerie with rose petals on the bed and candles around my tub. I'm going to tell him to meet me so we can get something to eat, and if everything goes as planned, we'll come back here. I want you to set everything up while we're out."

"Jasmine, I don't want to put a damper on things but what if things don't go as planned?"

"Then, I guess it wasn't meant to be and better to know now than later."

"You're right about that. I'll meet you after work before you meet up with him, and we'll pick out something. Then I'll go set up everything."

Jasmine was working so much she didn't realize it was almost quitting time until Joyce asked her was, she working late. Jasmine finished up and went to meet Alley.

Jasmine and Ally were shopping and having a good time when Jasmine's cell phone rang. Answering it without looking at the caller ID and still laughing, she heard Kaisha's voice on the other end saying

"What's so funny?" "Oh, hey K." Ally just rolled her eyes and walked to another rack. The line was quiet for a short while before Kaisha spoke again, "I miss us hanging out." Jasmine had detected sadness in Kaisha's voice. She felt bad for Kaisha, because she knew homegirl didn't have many friends.

"We will hang out when you get here?"

"I'll be there next Friday. Let's go out to eat and go see a movie or something. Jasmine." "Yeah."

"Don't forget. I'm bringing my co-worker with me. Her name is Sharon, and she's cool. First time in a long time I've been able to click with another female. She's from Fayetteville, too. She just moved here after a bad break up with her boyfriend. She's moving back, because she wants to try and get him back. I told her to go for it. I'll have to work some while I'm there. You know, training her.

She has to be ready to work on her own in two weeks, so I'll be able to be there for at least two weeks." Jasmine heard Ally clearing her throat.

"Okay, Kaisha. I'll make room for you and your friend, but I got to go now. Me and Ally shopping for my hot date tonight."

"Girl, I can't believe you're finally dating again. But I'm happy for you. Will I get to meet him when I come?"

"Of course, silly. I'll introduce you to him. You'll be here for two weeks, dah. I'm not going two weeks without seeing my sweetie."

"Oh, he's your sweetie. I definitely got to meet this man."

"Jasmine!" Ally yelled. "You got some place to be, remember?"

"Okay, yeah. K, I got to go. I'll call you later."

An hour later they had finished shopping and Jasmine was on her way.

Jasmine went to meet Emmanuel for a dinner date and Ally went to get Jasmine's apartment ready. Jasmine had beat Emmanuel to the restaurant. She was so glad that she had got there first she needed time to calm her nerves.

She was getting ready to tell this man her secrets and opening her heart to him even more. "I hope I'm not making a mistake," Jasmine mumbled to herself.

"Making a mistake about what?" Emmanuel asked. Jasmine hadn't realized that Emmanuel had come in.

"Oh, nothing, baby. I was just thinking out loud." Emmanuel sat back looking at Jasmine.

"You look more beautiful every time I see you," he said.

"Thank you," she said. They were both about to speak at the same time.

"You go first," he said. "No, you go first," Jasmine had insisted.

"My conversation may take a little longer."

"Okay, then I'll go first." "You know we said once we felt we knew each other better, we would introduce each other to our families. Well, I feel it's time." He waited a moment before going on, "Do you agree?"

"I do," she said. Emmanuel blew out a sigh of relief.

"I'm glad you said yes, baby, because my mom is dying to meet you. She is driving me insane."

"My mom is ready to meet you, too. But before we go any further, there's something I need to tell you." He looked at her a little closer and asked," What's the matter, Jazz?

You sick or something? You are scaring me with the seriousness in your voice."

"No, I'm not sick but this is serious. I hope you understand. Why I didn't tell you this before? I felt like I had to wait and see if we were going to get serious."

"Okay, I'm really curious now," said Emmanuel. Jasmine took a deep breath and let it roll.

"You know I told you I have had sex once, right?"

"Yeah, I remember. What about it?" His mind was wondering. He didn't know what to think. Where was she going with this?

"Well, we didn't use protection." Jasmine closed her eyes and Emmanuel envisioned her, the woman he has fallen in love with, telling him something he didn't want to hear.

"But wait," she said. She wasn't sick, so what could it be? Emmanuel thought.

Jasmine, calling his name, had brought him out of his trance.

"Oh, sorry, Jazz. Go ahead."

"Like I was saying, we didn't use protection and I became pregnant. I have a two-year-old daughter. Her name is Destiny and that is who I go see every day after work. She is staying with my mother while I attend college."

Emmanuel just sat there for a minute while the relief rolled over his body.

"Finally," he said. "Jasmine, please, baby. Don't ever scare me like that again."

"Did you hear what I said, Emmanuel? I have a daughter."

"Yes, I heard you."

"You're not upset?"

"Why would I be upset?"

"Most men don't like dating women with kids."

"Well, I'm not most men. I'm Emmanuel and if I love you, how can I stop just because you have a daughter?"

Did he say he love me? Jasmine thought.

Emmanuel didn't mean to tell her this now. He didn't want to move too fast, but too late. It's out now. So be it. Jasmine was so happy.

She was jumping up and down in the restaurant. People were looking at her weird, but she didn't care. She looked at him and said,

"Let's go."

"Go where?" he asked. "Get in my car and find out. It's our time now."

151

Emmanuel didn't know what our time meant, but he sure hoped it was what he thought it was. Jasmine called Ally and told her everything was cool.

Then she stopped mid-step and, turning around to face Emmanuel, said to him, "On the other hand, Manuel, can you drive your car? I have one stop to make. Meet me at my house in one hour and I mean one hour. Don't be late."

"Cool," Emmanuel said. That was fine with him. He needed to go home and get an overnight. He would leave it in the car just in case he was wrong. But something was telling him he wasn't. Her body language and that look in her eyes were screaming at him.

Emmanuel had called Jasmine on her cell phone. "Hey, baby, I was just wondering do you need me to bring anything?" he asked.

"No, Emmanuel. All I need is you."

"Alright, I'll see in an hour then.

Chapter 22

Jasmine rushed in the house and stopped cold. Ally was in the kitchen finishing up. She couldn't believe her eyes. Ally had outdone herself.

"I think you are taking up the wrong field," Jasmine told her. Candles were lit all over the house. Rose peddles started from the front door all the way to the bedroom. The Jacuzzi tub was bubbling with Jasmine's favorite sweet pea scent. She had tears in her eyes.

"Ally, you did all this for me?"

"Yes, girl. You know you, my dawg. And Lord knows one of us got to have some fun. Malcolm still holding out on me. I guess I'm going to have to make the first step just like you. I still can't believe you're going through with this. You're shocking me day by day. You must really care for him."

"I do, and he handled finding out about Destiny like a champ. I was so scared. But we can talk about that later. I got to get ready for my date. Stay here until he gets here. I'm going to jump in the shower. Then get in the Jacuzzi. Please send him in and lock up."

Ally put on a Will Downing CD. Jasmine loved his contemporary jazz. Just as she was about to sneak another chocolate covered strawberry, the doorbell rang. Ally opens the door with a cheeseburger grin on her face.

Emmanuel smiled but lost some of his smile when he saw Ally.

"God don't look so disappointed. I'm leaving. She said to come to the bathroom when you get here. I'll lock up. Y'all kids have a good time now." Jasmine heard Emmanuel walking toward the bathroom, and she became a little nervous. Emmanuel knocked on the bathroom door. He could see a little light.

"Come in," Jasmine whispered softly. Just the sound of her voice was sending chills down his back. Emmanuel walked into the bathroom, and he almost lost his balance.

There stood Jasmine in the Jacuzzi tub glistering wet. Her pecan brown skin was smooth. Her breasts were the size of small oranges. She looked so amazing. She was so beautiful.

"Are you going to stand there all day, Mr. McBride or are you going to join me?"

He said, "I just want to look at you for one more second." She blushed. "You are beautiful, my love."

Two seconds had passed when Emmanuel began shedding all his cloths. First, his shirt. After his shirt hit the floor, Jasmine looked up and gasped. She knew his chest was solid, but she didn't expect to see all the rips and abs.

Wow! He looks like a god. His skin is so chocolaty; it makes me want to run my tongue all down his chest. She looked down and his sweatpants were gone. All she could see were the muscles in his long legs. She got wet instantly just thinking about being wrapped between his thighs.

Emmanuel was stepping his foot in the tub when Jasmine looked down and saw what Emmanuel was really working with. She almost fainted.

"What's wrong, baby?" hc said. "Are you alright?" "Yeah, I'm okay, I think. I got a little lightheaded." Oh, God, what have I got myself into? I didn't even factor in all this, she thought to herself.

Emmanuel sensed Jasmine's nervousness, and he knew what it was. He saw her reaction when he stepped in the tub.

"Jasmine, I know what it is. It's okay. I promise it's not as bad as you think. I promise I'll be gentle." She relaxed some and smiled and then blushed.

"I'm sorry. I'm new at this."

"Don't apologize. I'm not a pro at this either. Everybody thinks I am. People think because I was a football star that I slept around all the time, but I didn't. I've only been with one woman so relax now, and let's enjoy each other."

Jasmine poured Emmanuel a glass of wine that she had chilling on the side of the Jacuzzi.

"Let's toast to us," she said.

"To us." In the Jacuzzi, they washed each other, talked, and played around. Both of them were like kids and were just really having a good time. Then Emmanuel pulled Jasmine to his chest. She leaned her head back and rested it upon his chest. Emmanuel rubbed her nipples, and they reacted instantly. They became hard like little pebbles. She moaned, and he hardened. He rubbed her between her legs. Finding her pearl was so easy. She let out a soft moan.

"Emmanuel, I can't take this. I want you so badly. My body aches."

Emmanuel lifted Jasmine out of the tub and wrapped her in one of the towels that she had laid out for them. He dried her off and then dried himself. Jasmine led Emmanuel to her bedroom where candles surrounded her bed. It was a nice glow of light in the room; just enough light for them to see each other. Jasmine took Emmanuel's hand and placed it upon her chest.

"My heart is beating a mile a minute," she told him.

"It's okay to be nervous. I am, too." Jasmine stood on her tiptoes to kiss Emmanuel. And when he met her halfway, as soon as their lips had touched, it was as if a lightning bolt had hit, and they began to caress each other. Then they fell on the bed. He was stroking her, and she began to beg.

"Please, Emmanuel! I want you now." Emmanuel couldn't stand her begging. He wanted her so badly, too.

"Hold on, baby. Let me get my…" She interrupted him by pressing her finger to his lips. "I got some on the nightstand."

Emmanuel protected them and joined Jasmine on the bed. He looked into her eyes. He knew she could see the hunger in his eyes, because he could see it in hers. Just to make sure, he asked her one more time,

"Are you sure?" She responded by grinding her hips upon his and nodding her head seductively. He didn't waste any more time.

He gently pushed himself inside of her. She was so tight, and he thought he would explode right then and there. So, he held himself right there. He didn't move. He was letting her body adjust to his. Then he felt Jasmine move beneath him, and he began to stroke her. She sped up, and he was going crazy.

She was thrusting her hips upon him, and he was thrusting back. If he didn't get control of himself, he would be finished. Before he could finish his thoughts, Jasmine had flipped him over and now she was on top. She began riding him like she was a world-class champion cowgirl. She was stroking him and calling his name at the same time. Emmanuel was matching her stroke for stroke.

He couldn't believe how good she was making him feel. He looked up at her, and she looked like she was in heaven. When she leaned back, he was able to see her pearl. He started massaging it slowly at first. Then faster and faster. She started riding him harder and screaming out his name all at the same time.

He knew she was about to reach her peek, because he was about to reach his. So, he thrust his hips up off the bed to meet her thrust, and they both climaxed together.

Jasmine collapsed on Emmanuel's chest. She couldn't believe how good she felt. Lord, if I'm dreaming, please don't wake me.

"You're not dreaming, baby. We're as real as they come." Jasmine didn't realize she had said that out loud.

"It's okay. I feel the same way. That was better than my dreams."

"You were having dreams about me?"
Jasmine asked.

"Yes, I was." She laughed. "I'm glad, because you sure did keep me up countless nights." They both laughed. They spent the rest of the night talking and making love.

Chapter 23

As the sun's rays played across Jasmine's face, Emmanuel just laid there watching her. She started to stir in her sleep, and then she turned over and looked up into Emmanuel's eyes. She smiled.

She couldn't believe she made love to him all night long and enjoyed every minute of it.

"Hey there you. How you are feeling this morning?" said Emanuel, smiling.

"I feel wonderful," she answered, smiling back. I keep wanting to pinch myself, Jasmine thought. Can't believe I'm this happy."

Emmanuel looked at Jasmine.

"Yeah, I know exactly what you mean." Jasmine's stomach growled.

"I guess we worked up an appetite. What kind of breakfast foods do you have?"

She started giggling, nonetheless.

"You count cereal?" she said.

"Okay, that's cool. I'll go run to the grocery store and pick up something, and come back and fix my queen some breakfast," Emanuel said. Jasmine couldn't do anything but blush.

She just said,

"Okay, hurry back. I need a repeat of last night." He jumped back on the bed and pulled her into his arms.

"Why wait?" She pulled him down onto her. He reached for the condoms and protected them and joined them once again. He was enjoying watching the different faces Jasmine was making. Jasmine flipped Emmanuel over, looked at him and said,

"Baby, I want you to hit it from the back."

"Oh, shit. Now, you don't have to ask me twice." They rocked with each other, thrust after thrust. Jasmine was reaching her peek. She was getting louder and louder. One last thrust from Emmanuel sent them both over the edge, both collapsing into each other's arms. They fell back asleep. Then waking up an hour later, they were smiling.

"I think you were made for me," Emmanuel told Jasmine.

"Same here," Jasmine said, her stomach growling again.

"Okay, I'm going to get us some breakfast." Jasmine got up to get her a shower so she can help Emmanuel fix their breakfast. She looked at the clock and saw it was almost eleven thirty. Goodness, we've been in bed all morning. Glad I took today off, she thought. I didn't know how last night was going to go so

I took off just in case. Glad I did, because I had a wonderful time. Jasmine put on a Mary J. Blige CD, and she was jamming. She was feeling so good. While singing aloud with the music playing so loud, she almost didn't hear the doorbell rang.

She ran to the door and opened it. Jasmine stuck her head out of the door expecting to see Emmanuel, but instead she came face to face with the last person she thought she would never see again. Damon.

"What the hell are you doing here on my front doorstep?" Jasmine screamed. "Get your sorry ass away from here before I call the police. I don't want to see your damn face. I can't believe you," said Jasmine, bitterly angry and upset.

"What about my daughter?" Damon asked.

"What about her? You are two years too late, don't you think? Don't try and see my daughter without my permission, or you'll have hell to pay." Moments later, walking up the steps while humming and smiling toward Jasmine's apartment, Emmanuel could hear loud voices like someone was arguing. Emmanuel walked up the steps faster, because he recognized one of the voices as being Jasmine's.

Thinking to himself, What the hell? Reaching her apartment, he heard the end of the conversation about Jasmine's daughter, Destiny. He was shocked and a little surprised to see this man standing here talking about his daughter. Didn't Jasmine say she hadn't seen him since they were together?

But Emmanuel's shock wore off fast when he saw the guy all up in Jasmine's face. "Yo partner, get out of Jasmine's face like that." Jasmine gasped and turned around when she heard Emmanuel's voice. Damon had her so upset until she had forgotten that Emmanuel went to the store. She was relieved to see him. Oh, God, Jasmine thought to herself. I wonder did he hear us arguing.

"Look, man. I don't want any trouble. I'm just trying to find out about my daughter."

"You couldn't use a phone for that?" Emmanuel asked with a little hostility in his voice. Damon looked at Emmanuel trying to size him up and trying to see if he could take him if need be. "I don't have her number and who the hell are you, her guard dog or her little buddy, because I know she isn't giving up anything else?" Emmanuel couldn't get over the nerve of this guy. He took Jasmine by the arm and led her into the apartment while looking back at Damon. "When you learn how to show her some respect, then you can try this again." He gently closed the door in Damon's face. Momentarily, Damon stood there looking at the closed door.

This did not go as planned. The way that guy was touching Jazz, it was as if they were intimate with each other. Can't be. Not the Jasmine I knew. Damn, it has been two years. Am I too late? Damon thought to himself. I just wanted to let her know how sorry I am, and I want to try and make us a family. Guess I have to catch her without Mr. Whoever-He-Is. Jasmine was pacing the floor back and forth.

She felt Emmanuel come and put his arm around her. "Talk to me, Jazz. What's the matter?"

"I can't believe he has the nerve to show his face after all this time." Emmanuel thought it was good he wanted to be a part of his daughter's life, but only if he plans to stay in her life, and not go back and forth. I just

170

don't agree with the way he's going about it, Emmanuel thought to himself.

But how was he going to tell Jasmine this knowing how she feels right now?

"Baby," Emmanuel said softly. Hearing him call her that made her calm down just a little. He then turned her around. "Look, I hope you don't get mad at me for this, but I think it's a good idea for him to step up and help you with Destiny and be in her life.

I do think he went about it the wrong way. I think you should hear him out and if you want me to be there I will." S

he looked him in the eyes and said,

"You would do that for me, Manuel?"

"Of course, I would. So don't worry about it no more today. Let's go make our breakfast and enjoy our day? I'm looking forward to meeting Destiny. We'll decide how to handle that later. All I want to do today is be with you."

After eating their breakfast well brunch is more like it, they took a long shower together. Jasmine couldn't resist his offer of getting in the shower with him, and she didn't regret it.

As soon as she stepped into the shower, he took her in his arms and caressed her. He massaged every muscle she had, and some she didn't know existed. He made her feel good without even entering her. "God, a girl could get used to this type of treatment", Jasmine said within herself.

After a day of lovemaking and watching all kinds of DVD movies, they decided to go out and get some ice cream. On the ride there,

Emmanuel asked Jasmine, "What time do you go to bed? I know you have to work tomorrow, and I don't want to keep you too late." She looked at him and couldn't believe what she was about to say, but said it anyway,

"Emmanuel, would you like to spend the night again?"

He answered quickly, "I'd love to."

Walking back into Jasmine's apartment, she kicked off her shoes and flopped down on the couch. It had been a long day. Emmanuel went into the bathroom and before Jasmine knew it, she had dozed off to sleep and later, woke up to her favorite scent. She was looking around and was trying to figure out whether she'd fallen asleep with the water running. Then she looked up and saw Emmanuel, and she smiled. She hasn't yet gotten used to seeing him in her space.

"Come on, let's take a bubble bath." "Manuel, I'm going to turn into a prune. This is going to be my third time getting in water today."

"Come on," he pressed her. "I'll make it worth your while." "Okay," she said. "If you insist." After all, how can a girl turn down a challenge like this? She mused.

Getting into bed, Jasmine was exhausted. She hadn't gone to work, but almost two days of making love to Emmanuel made her fatigued.

Lying there beside Emmanuel, her mind drifted to opening her door and seeing Damon standing at her front door. Goodness, how she despised him right now? How could he not be in his daughter's life for two years, and then just pop up like he just went to the corner store for bread and milk? Ugh, the nerve of him. Emmanuel looked over at Jasmine and saw that she was deep in thought.

"What's the matter, Jazz? You look like you're a thousand miles away."

"I was just thinking about how Damon showed up here today, but I don't want to think about it anymore. One of my friends, Kaisha is coming home for a visit this Friday, and I want you to meet her. I'm going to warn you beforehand. Kaisha and Ally are not getting along right now. I'm not going to go into the reason right now, but it's kind of big. So don't be surprised if they seem kind of cold towards each other. She is bringing a coworker with her, and they are going to stay here while they're here in town."

"That's cool," Emmanuel said. "I look forward to meeting your friend, and when I want to steal you away you can come to my place."

"Oh, that sounds nice," Jasmine said. "I'm looking forward to that."

"Don't be getting excited. I might take you home and don't bring you back." Jasmine was laughing and Emmanuel said "You laugh and

I'm for real. We'll go get Destiny and go to my place and just chill."

It took a minute to realize what Emmanuel had said to her. Her and Destiny.

"Damn you, Damon", Jasmine said to herself. How in the hell do I introduce her to two men at once? Even though I hate it, I'm going to have to wait and hold off introducing Emmanuel to Destiny.

"Jasmine!" Emmanuel called out to her. "Where you go this time?"

"Just thinking. We'll talk about it later. You ready for bed?" she asked.

"Sure, I'll just hold you close tonight. Seems like you got a lot on your mind. I'm ready to talk whenever you are."

"Thanks, Manuel. I'm glad you're here tonight." As soon as Jasmine's head hit the pillow, she was out. Emmanuel admired her for a few minutes, and then he was off to sleep, too.

Chapter 24

When Jasmine woke up the next the morning, Emmanuel was gone. She started to panic until she heard him coming through the front door. He had gone jogging; he looked so sexy with the sweat running down his face. His wet T-shirt was sticking to his chest, and his abs looked so delicious.

Jasmine started having flash backs, and the heat of passion became apparent in her eyes. Emmanuel saw it and started taking off his clothes right there in front of her. She just stood there and watched him. He walked towards her until he was standing right in front of her. She couldn't get over how gorgeous his body was. She couldn't believe how he set her body on fire. Emmanuel took Jasmine by the hand and led her to the bathroom where he took off her clothes.

Then he turned on the shower water. He knew Jasmine had to go to work this morning. He was just glad it was still early. He steps into the shower bringing her with him. She bathed him slowly and caressed his body gently.

He lifted her up and placed her against the wall tile. He wanted her right then and there, but he knew he had to protect them, so he was about to stop until Jasmine told him that it was okay if he wanted to.

"I've been on the pill for two years to keep my cycle regular," she continued. Emmanuel looked at Jasmine, and asked her whether, she was sure. She knew exactly what he was really asking, and then shook her head.

"Yes, I'm sure," she told him. He entered her with one quick thrust, and she was rocking her hips to match his. After a few strong hard thrusts, they fell into each other's arms.

After finishing their shower and eating breakfast, Jasmine called her mom to check in on Destiny. Destiny answered the phone as usual. "Hello," she sang into the phone.

"Good morning, Destiny. It's –" Before Jasmine could fully identify herself, Destiny was yelling, "Hey, mommy!"

"Hi, Destiny. How are you this morning?"

"I'm being good for Nana. She's in the kitchen cooking us some breakfast. Are you getting ready for work, mommy?"

Jasmine thought for a moment that this girl is one smart two almost three-year-old.

"Yes, Destiny. I'm getting ready for work. I'm leaving as soon as I talk to your Nana."

"Nana, my mommy on the phone," Destiny yelled. Jasmine could hear her mother before she got to the phone, because she was singing

Amazing Grace, which she sang ever since Jasmine was a little girl.

"Good morning, Ma. How are you doing today?"

"I'm good. How did your date go? I didn't hear from you so I'm assuming it went alright. Did you tell Emmanuel about Destiny?"

"Yes, I told him, and he was wonderful. Very understanding and he is ready to meet her and you. He wants me to meet his family. Are you sitting down, because something else happened to me?

Emmanuel had gone to the store, and the doorbell rang a few minutes after that. I thought it was Emmanuel. I open the door, and it was Damon standing there. We got to arguing. He was talking about what about his daughter. Ma, he pissed me off so bad. I had forgotten Emmanuel was even gone to the store until he got back and heard me and

Damon arguing. He asked him to leave, and then told him when he had learned to talk to me respectfully; he can then try this again. What am I going to do? How do I introduce her to her dad and my boyfriend at the same time? She will be so confused?"

"First thing's first, with Damon I will not and yes, I said I will not have him hurt you or Destiny again. We will get in touch with him. I'm sure he's at his mom's, and we will find out what his intentions are. We will allow him to see her a day or two at first, but we will not tell her that he's her father until we're sure that he's on the up and up. Something has brought him back here. I'm not sure what it is, but I'm sure it's not Destiny. I got this strange feeling that something's about to go down. We got to watch him carefully."

"Okay, mom. We can talk about it more when I get there after work. Oh, yeah. Before

I forget, Kaisha is coming on Friday. Her and a coworker that she has to train."

"Okay, it will be nice seeing her again. How is Alicia handling her coming?"

"She's dealing with it for me, so that's all I can ask of her right now."

"I'll cook dinner for all of you. You invite Emmanuel over, and Alicia and her friend."

"Thanks, mom. This will be a great turnout. A nice get together for everyone. Alright, I got to get out of here. I'll see you this evening."

"Kaisha, I really appreciate you training me. I know it can be a pain having someone follow you around all day, but I needed this training to transfer back home. Like I told you before, I'm trying to get back with my ex-boyfriend. I made a mistake and cheated on him, and now he won't even accept my phone calls or talk to me. I'm hoping I can change his mind when I see him in person. Maybe by me being back in town, he will have second thoughts. One of my friends said she saw him hanging out with some skinny girl, but I doubt it's serious. If it is, then I don't mind playing dirty to get him back."

"I agree," Kaisha said, "but be careful. I fought dirty, and I lost the one man that I loved and almost lost my best friend in the process. So be careful."

"Oh, do tell," Sharon asked her. "I knew we kicked it off for a reason."

"Well, to make a long story short, I went after someone and even though he was getting married, I didn't care. However, it didn't work out between us. I try not to think about it too much, because it makes me sad.

 "I'm going to try and make things work with Mike."

"I'm with you, trying to get your man back. If you need my help, let me know. I'm going to call Jasmine and make sure everything is still set with us staying with her. I'll get back with you later, and let you know what's what." Jasmine was cruising and listening to her Heather Hedley CD. Her cell phone was ringing, interrupting her morning groove. Looking at the caller ID, she saw it was Kaisha. She started to send her to voicemail so she can continue getting her morning groove on, but knowing Kaisha the way she did, she'll just keep calling until I answered.

So, I might as well answer.

"Hello, Kaisha." "Hi, Jazz. I just wanted to make sure it was still okay for me and Sharon to stay with you while I'm there." "Everything is set. My mom is cooking dinner for you so when you get in town, we'll be going over there. You'll finally be able to meet Destiny."

"Who's Destiny?" "That's my daughter, Kaisha. You've missed out on a lot since you left and didn't contact anyone."

"Oh, Jazz. I'm so sorry. You mean I got a goddaughter and didn't even know it?"

"Well, Alicia is her godmother. She was there with me through everything that I went through with Damon and being pregnant alone. So, when you get here, it's not up for debate. You can be Auntie Kay."

"Okay, that sounds good, too."

"Okay, I'm at work now so call me before you board the plane on Friday."

"I can't believe that in one day, I'm going to be back in the Ville," Kaisha said.

"Seem kind of eerie a little bit." Jasmine said "Before I go, I want to ask you something. Are you going to see your mom?"

"Why?" The line went silent.

"Alright, I was just asking. Call me when you board."

"Alright, talk to you then." Jasmine didn't want to push Kaisha, but she really thought she should go see her mom. There's a lot they needed to get out in the open. Walking into the office, Jasmine said, "Good morning" to Joyce.

"Good morning to you, Ms. Lady. How are you? Are you feeling, okay? You took off work yesterday." Joyce had this little smirk on her face. She already knew what was up.

"Oh, yeah, I was a little under the weather, but I'm definitely better this morning."

"Well, I'm glad to hear. I guess Emmanuel was worried about you, too, because he left you a message to call him. He said he tried to call your cell but got a busy signal."

"Thanks, Joyce. Let me go call him now."

"Yeah, you do that," Joyce said, smiling and shaking her head. Jasmine called Emmanuel. While waiting for him to answer, her mind drifted to Damon and what he was really up to.

Emmanuel answered the phone sounding a little short winded.

"Hey, boo," he said. "I was just working out." Just the vision of him working out was getting Jasmine all hot and bothered. "Jazz!"

188

"Oh, sorry, Manuel. My mind was wondering."

 "On me I hope."

"You know it. I was just returning your call. Joyce told me you called." "My mom wants you to come to dinner on Saturday. You think you can swing it with your girlfriend coming into town?" "Yeah, I should be able to get away for a little while on Saturday. Wait Manuel, can you ask your mom if we can do it on Sunday? I want to take Destiny out Saturday, and I think that is when we may let Damon see Destiny."

"Okay, will do. I don't think that would be a problem as long as she gets to meet you."

"Good. Just let me know the time, and I'll be ready. Let me go. I got a lot of work to do. Kaisha will be here tomorrow, so I need to get a little ahead."

"Okay, talk to you later."

Chapter 25

Ally was enjoying her relationship with Malcolm. It has been a long time since she had felt this happy. Since her break up with Stephen, she hasn't really dated much. Malcolm has brought so much joy into her life. She was ready to take their relationship to the next level.

When the doorbell rang, it brought Ally out of her daydream of Malcolm. She wasn't expecting anyone, so she peeped through the peephole and started laughing when she saw Jasmine.

"What are you laughing at?" Jasmine asked after Ally had opened the door laughing. Jasmine entered Ally's place.

"I was peeping through the peephole, because I wasn't expecting anyone. I didn't feel like being bothered by my neighbor asking me for any more milk."

"Girl, your ass is crazy. Give that woman some milk. You know you aren't going to drink it anyway."

"Hush, what are you doing here anyway?"

They both sat down on Ally's sofa together.

" Girl, you would never believe who showed up on my front doorstep?"

"If I didn't know better, I would say Damon. But I know it isn't him so who was it?" Alicia waited for Jasmine to answer her, but she never did.

Ally said, "I said, who was it, Jazz?" Tears were rolling down Jasmine's face, and in that moment, Alicia knew it was Damon who had showed up on Jasmine's doorstep. Alicia reached over to Jasmine and gave her a hug.

"Oh, Jazz. I'm so sorry. I know you're reliving what you went through. Don't give him that power. You have come so far. Don't back track now. You got a great guy in your life now. We will get through this just like we did before. Did he say why he was back?"

"No. Just said he wanted to see his daughter. This is going to be complicated. I just decided to introduce her to Emmanuel. How do I introduce her to two men at one time? She'll be as confused as I am right now. Momma is mad. She thinks he is up to something." "I do, too, because he doesn't even call his momma to check on Dee." "We're going to let him see her, but we are not going to tell her that he's her dad, not until we are sure what he plans to do. If he can't agree to that, he can take me to court. He will not hurt my baby like he hurt me."

"Don't worry, Jazz. With me, momma and Emmanuel on your side, everything will be fine."

"Alright, I'm going to go so I can get the spare room ready for Kaisha and her friend."

"Good luck with that."

"Be nice. You promised."

"Well, she isn't here yet."

"Bye, Ally. I'll call you later."

Emmanuel phone was ringing he answered his cell phone without looking at the caller ID. As soon as he heard who was on the other line, he knew he had made a mistake.

"What do you want, Sharon? I told you; I was with someone else. There's nothing for us to talk about. Please stop calling me. You wanted your football player. He used you and dumped you. Now, you want to come back. No sir, keep stepping. I don't want to see or talk to you. Goodbye."

After hanging up the phone, Emmanuel said to himself, "I got to tell Jasmine about Sharon calling me just in case she calls again, and we're together. Because I know I haven't heard the last of her."

Jasmine got home and was getting ready to take a shower when her doorbell rang. She grabbed her bathrobe and was rushing to the door in hopes that it was Emmanuel. Looking through the peephole, she quickly saw her hopes go up in smoke. She couldn't believe her eyes. It was Damon at her front door. Again! What the hell does he want now? She opened the door just a little, just enough to poke her head through. As soon as Damon saw her face, he put on a fake smile.

"Hi, Jazz," he said. "How are you today?"

"Don't call me that," Jasmine said, thinking that her ex had to be the devil incarnate standing at her front door. She suddenly developed a sick feeling, right in the pit of her stomach. "That's reserved for my friends."

"Look, Jasmine. I didn't come here to argue. I came to see if I could talk to you about Destiny. I know I did wrong, but I want a chance to make up for not being there. I can't change the past, but I can try and work on the future." Jasmine just looked at him like he was crazy. She wanted to say so many things to him, but the cat had her tongue. He was really laying it on thick. She had to get him away from her. She needed her mom whenever she was dealing with Damon.

"Damon, why didn't you call? If you can find out where I live, you can also find out my number. Can you come by Saturday and see Destiny? We are not going to tell her you're her father yet. We want her to be able to warm up to you first. Then we'll go from there."

He thought for a minute and then agreed that it was fair. "I'll see you Saturday, and Jasmine."

"Yes."

"You look wonderful." Jasmine just looked at him and closed the door. She didn't want to hear none of that bullshit. This was about Destiny and Destiny only. Jasmine went and ran her bath water. Her mind was spinning a mile a minute. She didn't know how she was going to get through this weekend. First, Kaisha and her coworker were coming to town. Kashia and Ally are not getting along. Destiny will be meeting Damon, and I will be meeting Emmanuel's parents. Emmanuel is meeting mine. All I can say is, Lord, give me the strength. Before she knew it, Jasmine had fallen asleep in the tub. She woke up in cold water and a ringing cell phone. Answering the phone, she smiled when she heard Emmanuel's voice.

"Hi, sweetness," he said. "How are you?"

"Better now that I'm hearing your voice. I miss you already."

"I miss you, too. What time are you heading to bed?

"In about an hour or so," she answered.

"Why, do you want to come over since Kaisha and her friend will be here tomorrow?"

"Yes, I'm on my way," Emmanuel said quickly. "I'll be there in about ten minutes."

"You must be close to here."

"I am. I was hoping to get an invite. I wanted to see you and talk to you about something."

"Okay, I'll see you when you get here. Be safe."

Several minutes later, Emmanuel rang the doorbell. Jasmine let him in. She had on a red teddy. Emmanuel just stood there leaning on the door and looking at her. He didn't think he would ever tire of looking at her. She was so beautiful. She had no idea how beautiful she was. Jasmine gave Emmanuel a look that he was becoming familiar with. That look that says she wanted him. Then, that look made him want her more than she wanted him. He knew it would probably be a while before they had some alone time since her friend will be here for two weeks. So, he didn't waste any time picking Jasmine up and taking her to the bedroom, and then laying her down. He wanted to take his time pleasing Jasmine tonight. He wanted her to know how much she meant to him. He wanted her to feel his every emotion when he made love to her tonight.

He caressed her gently and she purred like a kitten. He was stroking her so tenderly and slowly. It was as if he was peeling away layer by layer to get to her heart. Jasmine thought to herself that Emmanuel was taking her to places she had only dreamed of and read about in her romance novels. Jasmine had no idea she could ever feel this way. She just moved her hips to their slow grind while the tears of pure ecstasy rolled down her face.

Emmanuel continued to stroke Jasmine until he couldn't take it anymore. She had already reached a climax two or three times, and he couldn't hold it any longer. He held her tight and whispered in her ear, "Jasmine, I love you." His climax rocked his body so hard until he knew he couldn't let Jasmine go.

He wanted her forever. Sleep was falling upon both of them fast. Not wanting to ruin the mood, he decided to not tell her about Sharon calling him. He'll tell her later. With that, he kissed her good night and they fell fast asleep in each other's arms.

Chapter 26

Waking up together was feeling better and better to Jasmine and Emmanuel. They jumped up quickly, because Jasmine's cell phone was ringing constantly. She knew it couldn't be anyone but that damn Kaisha calling back-to-back like that. She must be getting ready to board the plane.

Jasmine answered the phone.

"Yes, missy."

"Jasmine, what took you so long answering the phone? You must be busy with your mystery man." Jasmine just laughed. "Oh, yeah, I got to meet this gentleman that got you acting like this. But anyway, I'm getting ready to get on the plane. Me and Sharon will be there in about an hour. So, see you then. I'll let you get back to whatever you were doing."

"I better let you get ready baby. Sounds like you will have company soon. Let's go jump in the shower and go get some breakfast, and then you can get your friend from the airport. And I guess I will see you on Sunday when you meet my parents."

"Oh, I almost forgot, my mom wants to meet you tonight. She is having a coming home dinner for Kaisha, and she also wants Ally and Malcolm to come, too. I hope momma knows what she is doing. This is going to be an eventful night."

"That sounds nice. I'll be there with bells on," Emmanuel said. "While we are talking, I wanted to let you know Sharon's being calling me and wanting me to see her, and I just wanted to let you know just in case she be ringing my phone off the hook and we're together.

I just didn't want you to be wondering why I'm not answering my phone."

Jasmine looked Emmanuel in the eyes, and asked him point blank, "Do I have anything to worry about?" He looked her in the eyes and told her, "No, not one thing."

"Okay, well I consider the case closed. Let her call. If it gets too bad, block her number. You can go in your phone or call your carrier and they will block her number."

"Good idea," Emmanuel said. "I think I'll do just that." They both showered quickly and went to get breakfast. Standing between their cars at the diner, Emmanuel told Jasmine,

"Okay baby, I'll see you tonight. Have fun with Kaisha." He kissed her and got in his car.

Then Jasmine headed to Fayetteville Regional Airport to pick up Kaisha and Sharon. While Jasmine waited for Kaisha, she called Alicia who answered the phone on the first ring. She was just getting off the phone with Malcolm. "What up, Jazz?" Before Ally could say anything else, Jasmine had jumped in, "Don't forget about tonight and don't be late. You know how mama is. Momma wants you to bring Malcolm so she can meet him. And behave tonight, too. No arguing. No fussing. Oh, but not to worry cause momma will set y'all straight and keep y'all in line. Tell Malcolm not to worry because he won't be by himself. Emmanuel will be there, too."

"So what time is Kaisha's flight due in?"

"She should be here in about another twenty minutes.

Why? You want to come down and help me welcome her home."

"Hell no! I don't want to come down there. You lucky I agreed to hang out period. You know she gets on my last nerve.

I should have never let her in my wedding party. It was doomed before it began fucking with her."

"Alicia!"

"Yeah, I know. This is what she brings out of me. Ugh! This is going to be a long two weeks. I know you want to believe in Kaisha. I just hope she doesn't hurt you before you find out what kind of person she really is. It is so obvious that she is jealous of you. You want to see the good in everyone, but you're overlooking the one person that could cause you the most harm. I'm going to stop. I'm not going to mention it again. All I can say is watch your back. You now have a man. Please keep him close."

"Ally!"

"I'm just saying I don't trust her."

"Okay, point taken. I think it's about time for Kaisha's plane to land. I'll see you tonight," Jasmine told Alicia.

"Alright, I'll call Malcolm and let him know we are invited to dinner. I'm sure he won't have a problem with it. He loves to mingle and get to know people. Before I go, I'm warning you.

If she so much as look in Malcolm's direction, I'm going to let her ass have it."

"She's not going to do anything, Ally. She's trying to mend fences, not break them."

"Okay, let's hope you're right. You're her biggest cheerleader. Let's hope you're not cheering for a losing team." Jasmine heard someone call her name. Then she turned around and saw Kaisha coming her way.

"Okay, bye, Ally. Kaisha is here. I'll see you tonight." Kaisha embraced Jasmine.

It had been two years since they last saw each other. While hugging her, Kaisha's mind started to waiver because part of her loved Jasmine and other part hated her. Kaisha hated Jasmine for what she had and for what she herself didn't have.

No one knew what Kaisha had found out, and she couldn't tell anyone because it would only make her look more like a fool. So, she had to keep that part of her that hated Jasmine to herself as well as that part of her who wanted to make Jasmine miserable. She had to keep all her feelings at bay. Sharon cleared her throat to get Kaisha's attention.

"Oh, I'm sorry. Sharon, it's just been a while since I've seen Jasmine. Well anyways, Jasmine this Sharon and Sharon this Jasmine."

"Nice to meet you, Jasmine."

Sharon was looking Jasmine up and down. She knew this could not be the girl Emmanuel was dating. Naw couldn't be she thought, but she looks like the girl in the picture her cousin sent her of them at the jazz club. What could he see in her? Her eyes are big, and she looks like a choirgirl. Oh, this is going to be like taking candy from a baby." Sharon thought to herself "

"Something wrong?" Jasmine asked, bringing Sharon out of her trance.

"Oh, no. You just look a little familiar, that's all."

"Oh, well. You know what they say, everyone has a twin."

"Yes, that's true," Sharon had said. "It's nice to finally put a face to the name. Kaisha has told me so much about you. I feel I know you already."

Jasmine developed a strange feeling like Sharon was trying to be funny. Some introduction. Oh, well. Whatever Jasmine thought.

"Jasmine, what's on our agenda? I know your mom is cooking tonight, but before then what are we getting into? If nothing is planned, I would like to go by the flea market. I miss the flea market, and I am dying to get me some of those homemade doughnuts. Is Dwight still selling CDs in the flea market? I can pick me up some tunes."

"Tunes," Jasmine said. "Yes, you definitely been gone too long." Kaisha just burst out laughing. Sharon was walking between them, but her mind wasn't on their conversation. It was on finding out if indeed this was the girl in that picture. I guess only time will tell, Sharon thought. And if it is, she can't wait to see Emmanuel's face. With that thought, Sharon got happy. She couldn't wait to see if this would be her lucky day. She couldn't wait to see if this little lady would lead her right to Emmanuel.

"Boy, I sure do feel like shopping now," Sharon suddenly spoke. She thought she would make nice with Jasmine to what information she could get from her. Sharon started talking and laughing more with Jasmine and Kaisha. Although they both were making her sick on the stomach, she had to keep up her front. She had to know if Jasmine was Emmanuel's so called 'New Girl'. Ugh, I'll see about that, Sharon pondered in her heart.

"Jasmine, can we go by the mall? I think I want to get something a little sexy to go under my clothes. I love to feel sexy. Never can tell when a quickie might hit you." Kaisha and Jasmine looked at each other.

"Guess you got some plans."

"Oh, I do hope so, but time will tell soon enough," Sharon said, wearing a cheesy grin on her face.

Walking out of the mall, Kaisha said, "I'm good and hungry now. Jasmine, I'm ready for some of momma's cooking. It doesn't seem like we been in that mall for four hours. Hope we all still got money left in the bank." They all started laughing.

"Kaisha, I'm going call Ally and see if she's on her way." Moments later, Ally answered the phone quickly.

"Yes, mama," Ally said, sarcastically on the other end of the line.

"Are you on your way yet?" "Yeah, I just picked up Malcolm and we're on our way."

"Okay, I'll see you there." Jasmine hung up and called Emmanuel.

"Hello, sweetness," Emmanuel said as soon as he answered the phone.

"Hi," Jasmine answered back. "I was just checking to see if you were on your way."

"I'm almost finished getting dressed and I'll be right over."

"You still got the address?" she asked.

"Yes, I got it. I should be there in about twenty to twenty-five minutes."

"Okay, I'll see you then. Drive safe," Jasmine said.

"Ok, I love you."

"I love you, too." Sharon jerked her head up so fast that this action almost gave her a serious neck cramp. Did she just say I love you, too? Sharon said within herself. What the hell? They've been dating all a hot minute and he's talking love. Oh, hell naw!

I got to move quickly before this goes any further. I got to think fast. I need something that's going to send her ass packing and not look back. Sharon thought to herself.

Sharon was so deep in thought that she hadn't even noticed them pulling into Jasmine's mom's driveway.

"Kaisha, you and Sharon can go on in the house. I got to get some things out of the trunk." Kaisha and Sharon had exited the car and walked up to the front door. Kaisha knocked at first but afterwards, she let herself into the house with Sharon following close behind.

When Linda spotted Kaisha over at the bar, she came around and gave her a hug.

"Nice to see you again, Miss Lady."

"Same here," Kaisha said. "This is my friend, Sharon. We work together, but she is originally from here, too."

"Oh, really? Who your people?" Linda asked.
"The Butlers," Sharon answered.

"The Butler's from Belt Boulevard?"

"Yes," Sharon said.

"Oh, okay. I know some of them. We went to school together." "Kaisha, where's my baby girl?"

"She com…"

"I'm here," Jasmine interjected, walking through the front door carrying bags, before Kaisha could finish her sentence. Walking straight into the living room, Jasmine continued, "I'm here, momma." It made Kaisha insanely jealous and sick to see Jasmine and her mother interacting in harmony. She hated that she and her own mother didn't have a close relationship, but it's her own fault! Kashia felt she would never forgive her for what she done to her.

"Mommy! Mommy!" was the next thing Kaisha heard. She turned around and saw a small Jasmine. She was so beautiful, and in that moment, envy had filled Kaisha's heart. Lord, will this ever go away? Kaisha thought. "How's my big girl? Have you been a good girl for grandma?"

"Yes, mommy. Mommy, you know I'm always a good girl for grandma. Who dat lady, mommy?"

"That's mommy's friend, Kaisha."

"Oh, I remember you talking to her on the phone." "She and her friend, Ms. Sharon will be visiting with us for a couple of weeks."

"Yes, that's right" Kaisha jumped in.

"Do you like to read?" Destiny asked Kaisha. "I love to read."

"Yeah! can you read me a story?"

"Yes, I would love to read you a story." Kaisha said.

Sharon was watching Jasmine. She couldn't believe Emmanuel was talking to someone with a child.

"Ugh he must have gotten desperate since I left him. But I can change all that. All I must do is remind him of what we once had, and he will be mine again. And she'll just go back to wherever she came from." Sharon thought to herself.

The doorbell rang and Sharon got nervous. She was hoping to come face to face with Emmanuel. But instead, in walks a girl who I could tell she thought she was the shit. Then behind her was that fine-ass Malcolm. Yep, it's confirmed. It's Emmanuel. They are dating friends. Yes, I'm ready. Let's see how he gets through this one. Sharon thought to herself.

When Ally looked up and saw Kaisha, all the dislike she had for her hit her like a ton of bricks. Ally prayed inwardly, Lord, give me the strength to get through this night. Just then Destiny jumped off the sofa where Kaisha was reading to her and ran to Ally.

"Hey, Na Na." This was Alicia's nickname that Destiny gave her.

"Hi, little girl. How are you doing?"

"I'm doing good. Ms. Kaisha was just reading me a story." Alicia looked at Kaisha again, and she looked pissed off. You could just tell by her look. "I see nothing has changed so I'm going to be the bigger woman," Ally said to herself.

"Hello, Kashia. How are you doing? It's good to see you." Alicia looked at Kaisha and said,

"Hello, how are you?" "I've been good. Good to be home. I look forward to us hanging out." Alicia knew she was trying to be funny, so she just went with the flow until Kaisha said, "So who is this nice gentleman here?"

Jasmine saw the look in Ally's eyes, and she quickly intervened.

"This is Malcolm. He is Emmanuel's friend. Emmanuel is my boyfriend," she said, blushing. Sharon's head popped up quickly.

Confirmed! Let's get this party started right! Sharon thought to herself. Emmanuel will be here in a little bit. I'm ready for his ass.

"Alicia, you want to help me in the kitchen? Mama, fix some finger foods. Help me bring them in the dining room."

Malcolm could feel Kaisha staring at him. He turned just to see, and he was right. She was smiling and looking. I see she's a piece of work, he thought. Let me get out of here. I got to get somewhere and warn Emmanuel that his worst nightmare is sitting in Jasmine's living room. He thought to himself.

Malcolm excused himself and went to ask Jasmine where her bathroom was. Moments later, the doorbell rang. Malcolm, knowing that it was Emmanuel at the front door, stopped and turned around.

He walked back into the living room, and moments later, Jasmine emerged from the kitchen to go open the door for her man.

Jasmine swung the door open with a smile on her face, but that smile changed within moments. Her mom had come out of the kitchen and saw the look on her daughter's face.

"What is it, Jazz? Honey, why you looking like that?" Jasmine didn't say anything, so Linda went to the door herself.

"What the hell are you doing here?" Linda said. "Didn't Jasmine tell you that you could see Destiny tomorrow?"

"Well, I heard you were having a coming home dinner for Kaisha and thought I could get introduced to Destiny while everyone was here. That way, it wouldn't be so complicated."

Jasmine just stood in the door looking at him. She wanted to curse his ass out, but her daughter was there so she had to be civilized.

She was fuming inside, but she stepped aside and let the slime ball in. I'm glad I met Emmanuel. If not, I'd probably think all men were scum, Jasmine pondered. I did think that until I met a real man. My man, Emmanuel McBride. Jasmine thought to herself.

As Jasmine was about to shut the door, she saw Emmanuel walking up the driveway. She was on cloud nine now. Her heart began beating fast. This man had her psyche all in knots.

"Hi, baby. Sorry I'm a little late. My mom needed me to run an errand for her right quick."

"That's okay. Dinner's not quite ready yet. Come on in so I can introduce you to everyone and oh yeah, Damon just popped up out of the blue. He is already trying to do what he wants to do."

"Calm down, baby. Don't let him ruin your day. Let's go have some fun."

Walking in the house, he saw his homeboy Malcolm and said, "What's up, man? Hi, Alicia. Good to see you again."

"Good to see you," Alicia said softly.

Alicia and Malcolm were acting kind of funny. He began to wonder what was going on. Then he turned around to meet Kaisha and came face to face with none other than his trifling ex, Sharon Black. And before he knew it, he had said, "What the hell are you doing here?"

Jasmine looked at Sharon and then looked at Emmanuel. Then it hit her. This must be his ex-girlfriend. She looked at Kaisha and said,

"Did you know about this? Did you know this was Emmanuel's ex?" Kaisha was speechless. She was just as surprised as everyone else, but Jasmine took Kaisha's silence as guilt.

"Get out!"

Jasmine "Wait!"

"I said get out!" Linda came out of the kitchen.

"What in the world is going on in here?"

"Sharon is Emmanuel's ex and Kaisha knew about it!"

Linda looked at Kaisha and asked, "Is that true, Kay? Did you do that?"

Before Kaisha could answer the question, Jasmine ran out of the door with Emmanuel on her heels.

"Jasmine, baby. Please wait, don't get in the car. I'll take you home. Just get in my car."

After getting into Emmanuel's car, Jasmine kept repeating, "I can't believe she would do this to me after all I've done for her. How she can be so heartless?"

Emmanuel just held her for a minute, long enough to calm her down. Then he took her to her apartment. When they walked into Jasmine's apartment, her message light on her phone kept blinking. But she didn't want to hear any messages tonight.

"Emmanuel, call my mom and tell her I'm safe please. I don't want to talk to anyone right now."

 "Okay, baby. I'll call. Go get out of your clothes, and I'm going to run you a hot bubble bath. Then we can talk. Stop worrying. We are going to work this thing out. You and me."

Chapter 27

Damon was glad he came by. If he hadn't, he would have missed the fireworks. He was still sitting down watching everyone move around Kaisha who was talking to Ms. Linda and trying to explain to her that she didn't know about the ex. She might not know, but I wouldn't put it past her. Jasmine still doesn't know to this day that Damon and Kaisha slept together. Boy if that ever came out. he tried to prevent it, but hell Kashia wanted it and she was pushing all Damon buttons. She knew Jasmine was inexperienced, so she used it to her advantage, and they were at it like rabbits for a while. Then she got possessive, and Damon had to cut her ass loose.

"Hello, my name is Sharon, and you are?"

Damon looked up. "Oh, nice to meet you, Sharon. I'm Destiny's father. I've just come back to town and wanted to see her.

 I guess you're the ex."

"Yes, trying to be the next," she said to herself. "So, you still got a thing for Jasmine?"

Damon looked at her strangely and said, "Meaning you still got a thing for Emmanuel."

"Yes, that is true. I thought maybe if you wanted Jasmine back, we could work together." Damon sat there for a moment. He really didn't want a relationship with Jasmine, but he sure would love to hit that again. She is looking fine as hell these days and with Mr. Man out of the way, his plans about Destiny could go smoother.

He needed his plan to work. He needed that money, and he was going to get it. No one will stand in his way, he thought to himself.

"So, what you got in mind?" he asked Sharon.

"We can cause problems between them. Put a wedge between them. Then when they're upset with each other, there will be our opportunity to strike. We got to use something good. Can't be mediocre. Emmanuel is a standup guy. It really must be something to ruffle his feathers." Hell, that's how I got away with cheating so long, Sharon thought to herself. "Okay, well, we better break this up. Let's exchange numbers and meet up tomorrow."

Sharon then walked over to where Kaisha and Ms. Linda were talking.

"Ms. Linda, if I may say something." Linda looked at her.

"Is it worth hearing?" she said. Linda was mad as hell. Jasmine was her baby. Even though she was grown, she was still her baby, and she was not going to stand by and let anyone hurt her.

Sharon swallowed hard.

"This was all a coincidence," she lied. "I didn't know Jasmine and Emmanuel were dating. Kaisha had no knowledge that I used to go with Emmanuel. Kaisha didn't know who Jasmine's boyfriend was until she walked through the door."

Ally chimed in, "I hope that's true, because Jasmine has always been there for you, Kaisha. And for you to have done something like that is really grimy. But I'm going to give you the benefit of the doubt. She's upset right now, and Emmanuel is with her. So, we will check on her tomorrow."

Alicia looked at Damon and said," I guess your introduction will have to wait, because we will not do it without Jasmine."

Damon always hated this goody goody bitch, but he played it off because he knew Linda would back her up.

He said, "That's cool. It's been a long night. I'll give her a call on Monday, and then we can set things up."

He did hate that he didn't even get a glance at Destiny, because of all the commotion. So, they sent Destiny to her room.

"I'm going to walk outside and get some air," Sharon said, following Damon out of the door.

While outside, Sharon started in, "So you are going to call me tomorrow so we can get this show on the road?" He looked at her and something was telling Damon to move on with his own plan by himself, and that getting into bed with this woman was going to be a huge mistake. But he needed to get in on Jasmine's good side and get Destiny. That is the only way he was going to get what was due to him.

"I'll call," was all he said to her. "Please try to be more discreet. All I need is for them to think we're in this together. I'll holla at you later," Damon said before getting in his car and driving off.

Sharon walked back into the house.

"Kaisha, do you want to get a hotel room?" Sharon asked.

"Yeah, let's go. Ms. Linda, I'll call you tomorrow."

Malcolm asked Alicia whether she was okay. She nodded a yes response and said, "I'm tired. Do you mind driving back to my place?"

"No problem." Malcolm then told Jasmine's mom, "Thanks for inviting him, and that he hated things ended the way they did. I was looking forward to some of your cooking. I hear it's something to talk about." She just started laughing.

"Would you like to take a plate for you and Alicia to eat later? I know she's upset, too. She and Jasmine are very close. They are just like sisters. When one hurts, the other does, too. They have been through a lot together, so you take care of my other daughter. And I'm going to go and fix y'all a plate to take home."

Before they could walk into Alicia's apartment, her neighbor had stopped her.

"This came while you were gone. It had a message if you weren't home for me to sign for it." Alicia looked puzzled. I wonder whom this letter could be from. She looked down and saw it was from Stephan. She dropped it and Malcolm picked it up. He saw the name and knew this was going to be a long night.

Alicia told him she hadn't heard from Stephan since she told him the wedding was off. So, he was wondering what this letter was all about.

Ally said, "He didn't even say goodbye. He just left the next day, and she hadn't heard from him until now."

"Come on, Ally. Baby, let's go inside." He opened the door and told the neighbor thank you. Closing the door behind them, he looked at Alicia and noticed she had tears gliding down her face.

"This night is just too much," she said. "Can you please stay with me tonight? I need you more than ever."

"Sure," Malcolm said. "Are you going to read the letter?"

"No, not right now. I just want to be in your arms right now and think of nothing else but you and me.

Kaisha and Sharon checked into the Hilton. They got a two-bedroom suite just in case they ended up staying there for their entire visit. They got settled in, and Kaisha was still upset.

"How can she think I would do that to her? What kind of person does she think I am?" Before Sharon responded to the questions, she thought to herself, *If I could flip this around, I could use this to my advantage.*

"If you ask me, Kaisha, I will say Jasmine doesn't have much faith in your friendship. If I was you, I wouldn't call her. I would let her call me. She must not consider you much of a friend. She wouldn't even let you explain. What kind of shit is that? I say move on with friends like that. Hell, you don't need no

234

enemies. I can tell that Mrs. Alicia thinks she is the next best thing since sliced bread. I saw the way she was looking at you. So, what's the deal? But before you answer that, I must tell you this Kaisha. Emmanuel is the guy I was telling you about. The one that I want back. He's the one I plan to get back." Kashia sat there for a minute.

Then she asked Sharon, "Do you want some help? I know how you can get Emmanuel back. If Jasmine thinks Emmanuel cheated on her, she will not take him back. There will be no ifs, ands, or butts so what do you say?"
"Let's teach her ass a lesson."

Sharon hadn't seen this side of Kaisha. Ever. It almost scared her. "Kaisha, are you sure you want to do this? This could be the end of your relationship if she finds out you helped me do this."

"She won't find out. No one will know but you and me. Then when she is all heartbroken, I'll be right there to help her pick up the pieces."

Sharon looked at Kaisha. Damn, this bitch is cold, she almost said aloud but caught herself. "I'm going to have to keep my eyes on her cause if she'll do that to her so-called best friend, she'll definitely fuck me over royally." Sharon thought to herself.

Malcolm ran a bubble bath for Alicia, and he decided to join her. He stepped in and she let out a gasp.

"You want me to leave?" he asked.

"No, I don't want you to leave. I want you to come over here and give me what I need."

"This is not how I planned for our first time to be but Malcolm, I need you. No slow stuff. Maybe later for that. I need you fast and hard.

I got so much pent-up frustration. I just need you to take me to another place."

Malcolm said, "Your wish is my command."

And just like that, he scooped her up and put her up on the shower wall. Then he entered her with one hard thrust. She wrapped her legs around his waist and bounced up and down with him. She was feeling so good, and Malcolm was doing a good job holding her up. That turned her on even more. They were having such a great time and were so caught up in their emotions that neither of them realized they didn't use protection. But it was too late by the time they thought about it because Malcolm had already exploded inside of Alicia. Alicia was breathing hard and coming down from her climaxed state.

"Ally, baby. I'm so sorry. I didn't protect us. I'm healthy I promise. I'll go get a test for you. I'm so sorry." "Calm down, Malcolm. It was both of our responsibility," she told him. "If you become pregnant, I'll take care of my responsibilities. I'm on the pill, Malcolm but if something happens, we'll deal with it when it comes up."

"I love you; Alicia and I want to be with you. I've never felt like this towards anyone before." Alicia was glad to hear Malcolm say these words, because she felt the same way about him and didn't hesitate to tell him.

They continued their shower, washing every inch of each other's bodies. Then later, they retired to Alicia's bedroom. Malcolm laid Alicia down on the bed and rubbed her body down with cocoa butter baby oil. Her skin felt so soft. He was rubbing her thighs, and he had to taste her. He couldn't resist tasting her sweet juices tonight. He opened her legs and massaged her clitoris with his thumb. She got wet instantly.

He replaced his thumb with his tongue, and he was branding Alicia as his woman for life. This is whom he wanted to be his wife one day. It hadn't been long since they've known each other, but he knew it deep down in his soul. And he planned on making sure she knew it, too.

"Malcolm, please. I can't take it no more. Make me yours again," she pleaded with him. Malcolm didn't worry about protection, because this would be his wife. He wanted all of her to himself.

While making love to Alicia, he had professed his love for her, and she did the same. Making love up to the wee hours of the morning, Alicia was sore because it had been a while for her. Lying in Malcolm's arms felt so right. She could get used to this. Maybe she'll even ask Malcolm to move in with her. She felt Malcolm kissing her cheek before he told her,

"Sleep tight, my love. I love you."

"And I love you, too, Malcolm."

Kaisha and Sharon sat up talking half the night about how they could come between Emmanuel and Jasmine.

"If I tell you this, you can't tell anyone ever. I know the perfect way to get what you want. All you have to do is get Emmanuel to his house, and I'll help you with the rest."

"Okay, I know just the way to do that."

"Well, I'm getting tired, and we got a lot of work to do tomorrow. Let's hit the sack."

"We will finish our plans over breakfast, my treat. You are the woman who's going to help me get my man back. It's the least I can do. Night, night, and don't let the bed bug's bite."

Kaisha fell fast asleep but was later awakened by one of her nightmares. The one where her mom didn't stop her boyfriend from having his way with her. What kind of mother lets her boyfriend have his way with her only daughter? she hated her ass with a passion. If her mother needed water to live, she would be a dead ass. Enough about her. I need to get back to sleep. Kashia thought. Kaisha got up out of bed and got her sleeping pills. She needed them more and more these days. She noted she needed to make an appointment with her therapist when she got back home.

Chapter 28

Jasmine woke up before Emmanuel. She decided to fix them some breakfast. She felt a little better than she did last night. Talking with Emmanuel helped a lot. She called her mom to check on Destiny and let her mom know she was doing well. Linda answered the phone on the first ring. She had been waiting for her baby girl to call.

"Hi, Ma. I'm sorry about last night. I don't know what happened to me."

"It's okay, Jazz. You were shocked to see Emmanuel's ex-girlfriend here with one of your best friends so it's okay. Just call her and talk to her."

"I will later. I just need to get my bearings together. I'm meeting Emmanuel's parents tomorrow. I'm trying to get my mind right for that, too. I'm going to call Alicia and let her know I'm okay, too. How is Destiny? I know she is confused."

"She didn't see you get upset, so she doesn't know anything is wrong. I told Damon that we would call him on Monday for him to see Destiny. I could tell he wasn't happy, but he said OKAY and went on his way."

"I'll be keeping an eye on him." She wanted to tell Jasmine to keep her eyes on Sharon. She was a woman on a mission, but she didn't want to upset Jasmine, so she kept it to herself. She felt Emmanuel was a good guy. He'll keep her in her place.

"Okay, Jazz. Go ahead and call Ally. Destiny is still sleep so I'm going to lay back down for a few."

Alicia answered the phone laughing, "Oh, you must have company. Am I disturbing anything?"

"No, Jazz. We're just getting up. What's up?

"Just wanted to let you know I was okay."

"I knew you were going to be fine. Emmanuel was with you. What are you doing up anyway calling people so early?"

"Just wanted to let you and momma know I was okay. Why don't you and Malcolm come over for breakfast, and let's spend the day together?"

"Hold on, let me ask Malcolm." Malcolm, standing behind Alicia, gestured a yes. He said, "That's fine. He wants to spend some time with Emmanuel anyway."

"Okay, I'll go wake Manuel and I'll have everything ready when y'all get here."

"Good, you only live around the corner."

Alicia got there in record time. Her and Malcolm were both hungry.

They had worked up a huge appetite. Emmanuel was in the kitchen helping Jasmine get breakfast ready. They worked so well together. Alicia just looked at them she told Emmanuel that he could go into the living room and talk to Malcolm. That she and Jasmine would finish up breakfast.

She really wanted to talk to Jasmine, and she knew Malcolm wanted to talk to Emmanuel.

"So now that we're alone, what are you going to do about Kaisha? Are you going to call her?"

"Not this weekend. I need to do some thinking. I'll call her on Monday. I have some things to think about. I may have jumped to conclusions and if I did, I need to reevaluate our friendship. For me to think that she would do that, I must not really trust her all that much. Maybe we have been a little hard on her Ally said."

"I want to be with you when you talk to her. Let's try and put this behind us. We need to feed our men before they starve to death."

"Malcolm, man, I was going to try and call you last night but as soon as I got up to call you, you were ringing the doorbell. I can't believe she is back, and I think she knew Jasmine was your girlfriend. I watched her. She didn't seem surprised to see you. It was like she was waiting for you to show up. You need to be careful. You know Sharon isn't playing with a full deck."

"Yeah, tell me about."

"Are you fellows hungry?"

"Yes, indeed," Emmanuel answered first, giving Jasmine that look. "I mean, for food, silly?"

"What are you talking about, boo? You know a brother hungry." They all ate breakfast and talked. Alicia became a little quiet at suddenly.

"What's wrong, baby? Why you get so quite?"

"I was thinking about last night." He smiled.

"No, before that." "The letter."

"Oh, that."

"What letter?" Jasmine asked.

"I received a letter from Stephan."

"Wow, you did. What did he say?"

"I haven't read it yet. I wanted you to be with me when I read it."

"Okay, we'll get the dishes done, go rent some movies, and then when we get back, we can read it."

"Ok buddy."

Sharon asked Kaisha, "Are you sure you want to help me?"

Now that Kashia had time to calm down and sleep on it, she really didn't want to do anything to hurt Jasmine, but she didn't want Sharon to think she was a wuss either. So, she went ahead with telling Sharon what they were going to do.

When she had finished telling Sharon what they were going to do, Sharon was happy.

"I think that would work with her out of the way. I can then make my move."

"Okay, we'll wait till later and then we'll put the plan in motion." Kaisha hoped this wouldn't come back and bite her in the ass.

She got away with this once doing it a second time and even the first time she had taken a big risk. But what the hell? Some people need to be brought down a peg or two, Kashia reasoned within herself.

Jasmine, Alicia and the guys had come back to the house with some great movies that they'd picked out for themselves, but now it was time to read the letter.

Alicia asked Jasmine to read the letter, and the guys asked Alicia whether she wanted them to leave but she said, "No, you can stay." She wanted…no, needed Malcolm to stay because she had no idea what was in the letter. Jasmine began reading,

"Dear Alicia, I hope this letter finds you in good health, mind, and spirit. I know you're wondering why I am contacting you after all this time. It has taken me some time to get over losing the best thing that has ever happened to me. I know you probably don't want to hear this or hear anything from me, but I just have to get this off my chest. I know I should have said something instead of just leaving when you told me it was over. But when I woke up with no clothes on and saw....

"What's wrong, Jasmine? Why you stopped?"

Jasmine sat down and said, "Oh, my God! I can't read the rest."

"If it's that bad, then I don't know if I can either. Malcolm, baby. Can you finish the letter?"

Malcolm looked at Jasmine. "If it's that bad, maybe she doesn't need to know what's in it. Maybe we should just throw it away."

"No, please finish reading. He must have thought it was something I need to know."

Malcolm took the letter and continued to read it....

"But when I woke up with no clothes on and saw... Malcolm stopped and looked at Jazz. .... And saw Kaisha lying there with nothing

251

on, I didn't know what happened. I didn't remember a thing. I was turned around and the next thing I knew, I woke up in bed with Kaisha. I knew you wouldn't forgive me when you found out Kaisha was the girl. I still don't know how you found out. I know Kaisha wouldn't have told you, because I truly do not know what happened. I hope we can be friends one day. Love Always, Stephan."

Alicia just sat there with tears running down her face. Jasmine was rocking her back and forth.

"Oh, Alicia. I'm so sorry. I'm going to kill her, Jasmine. Do you hear me; I'm going to beat her ass for the old and the new. And don't you try and stop me. She told me about a girl he was with. She never said that it was her. That little bitch! She wanted him for herself. That sneaky, conniving bitch!" Everyone was still in shock from the news of the letter.

They were sitting around trying to keep Alicia calm. Before they knew it, it had gotten so late, and Alicia and Malcolm decided to spend the night with Jasmine and Emmanuel.

Everyone was getting into bed when Emmanuel's cell phone went off. He started not to answer, but he recognized the number. It was the number from the security company.

"Hello, yes."

"May I speak to Mr. McBride?" the operator asked.

"This is he."

"We are letting you know the police was just dispatched to your home. It seems your alarm system has been cut. Are you away from home?"

"I am," Emmanuel said, "but I'm on my way." He knew in the back of his head that this had to be Sharon. It was so obvious.

So, he needed to deal with her once and for all, he thought. "Jasmine, baby. Something is wrong with my alarm system. I got to go check it."

"Do you want me to go with you?"

"No, you get some rest and get ready to meet my family tomorrow."

"I'll be going over there first thing to make my favorite pie for you and then I'll be here to pick you up."

"Okay, I'll see you tomorrow."

Emmanuel told Malcolm what was up. "I know its Sharon's ass acting a fool, but I'm getting ready to end this once and for all. I'll holla at you tomorrow and don't forget about dinner." They did their dap and Emmanuel left. Malcolm and Alley decided to still stay since it was late.

Emmanuel walked inside his house and turned on the lights. He heard a noise, turned around, and saw Kaisha.

"What are you doing in my house?" Before she could get anything out, Emmanuel felt a pain in his neck. He grabbed his neck and felt faint within seconds. Then everything went black.

"Oh, God," Kaisha said. "He wasn't supposed to see me. "What the hell am I going to do now?"

"Just calm down. Sharon said. We'll think of something. We're in this together."

Finale

Jasmine had awoken by her phone ringing. She almost thought she was dreaming. She had fallen asleep waiting for Emmanuel to call her. She must've not heard the phone ringing last night, and that he was calling early to wake her up.

She looked at the clock. It was already ten o'clock. Wow! She must have been tired. The phone was still ringing. She looked at the caller ID but didn't recognize the number. Should I answer it? She thought. It could be Damon. I don't want to talk to him, but on the other hand I can let him know to meet me on Monday.

"Hello," said Jasmine.

"Hi, my name is Geraldine. I'm Emmanuel's mother. He gave me your number in case I couldn't reach him on his cell."

"Oh, hi. I look forward to meeting you today."

"Well, that's why I'm calling. I been up waiting on Manuel, and he hasn't showed up. He wanted to cook something nice for you, but he hadn't showed up and I was wondering if he was there. He's not answering his cell or house number."

"No, ma'am. He's not here. He went home last night, because something happened to his alarm system and the alarm company had called."

"Oh, God. I hope nothing happened. I'm going to send his dad to his apartment."

"I will meet him there. Thank you for calling."

Jasmine ran and woke up Malcolm and Alicia.

"I think something might be wrong with Emmanuel. Let's go, I'll explain on the way."

Malcolm was driving so fast. He was scared for his friend. He was breaking all kinds of speed limits. Hopefully, no Fayetteville Finest was around right now to see it.

Pulling up the driveway, he saw Emmanuel's dad's car in the driveway.

"Emmanuel's dad is here. Let's hurry inside," Jasmine told everybody. Jasmine was out of breath by the time she got up the steps. They got to Emmanuel's door, and the door quickly flew open. Jasmine came face to face with her worst nightmare, Mr. James.

"Mr. James," she said, trying hard not to show him a surprised look.

"Jasmine, what are you doing here?" he asked, trying equally not to show his surprise. At that moment, all of Jasmine's hopes and dreams had flashed right in front of her eyes.

Oh, God. Is this real? What am I to do now? Jasmine walked inside the apartment and saw Emmanuel lying on the coach naked and Sharon in his shirt. "What the hell is going on here?" Jasmine yelled.

Mr. McBride said, "I was just asking the same thing. Why is my son not responding to me? What have you done to him?"

"He had too much to drink," Sharon lied.

Before Jasmine could say anything else, she couldn't even stop the thought before it entered her mind. I knew this was a love Too Good To Be True!

Upcoming Titles from Letitia Love

A New Journey Publishing

Ships to all Correctional Facilities

Place orders at A New Journey Publishing - Payhip

Made in the USA
Middletown, DE
27 February 2023

25636099R00156